Buffer Overflow

By Matthew Aadland

Matthew Aadland
matt@mjolnirpants.com

Table of Contents

Boot

Saturday, December 26th, 2759

Veridiboot 37.12.16 (Dec 26 2759 - 21:40:06 -0)

DRAM: 4096TB
MMC: quantic
Using default environment

In: bio-interneural/serial/wireless/quantic
nonserial
Out: bio-interneural/serial/wireless/quantic
nonserial
Err: serial
ATDP: network
IDPI: Bus 0: FAID 6 32475893434
                 Bus 1: network
UDP any packet to stop autoboot: 3... 2...
1... 0
reading bootimg
SCDI1: ...
                 All buffer addresses verified
4527888 terabytes read in 14 ms (308.4 ZeB/S)
reading u-boot.btl
SCDI2: Misaligned buffer address (00007fbfd90ba008)
10389 gigabytes read in 0 ms
setting up xQT6 zImage [0 - 4527888(10^9)]
[][] Traversed Device Architecture Tree at 00c0000a000f00
[][] Booting using the tdat at 0xc0000a000f00
Transferring control to operating system...

Viridian Dynamics CompanionSeries 7X Ver. 6.8 (build 902)
Copyright © 2752 Viridian Dynamics, Inc. All rights reserved.

System unexpectedly shut down, scanning for errors…
…
…
17 errors found. Repair queue updated. Errors will not preclude startup.
UDP any data packet to cancel startup: 3… 2… 1… 0.

Scanning for new hardware…
…
…
…
No new hardware found.
Scanning for new root-level software…
…
New root-level software found:
        Behavioral module 17c84f222a19000
Scanning new root-level software for malware…
…
…
…
…
…
No known malware found.
Scanning new root-level software for security flaws…
…
…
…

No security flaws found.
Loading new Behavioral module 17c84f222a19000…
…
Loaded. Warning: module size exceeds recommended root module size. Buffer overruns are likely to occur after 7600ms.
Booting now.

Awake

Saturday, December 26th, 2759

Amanda came to slowly. It was the smell that reached her first; hot garbage. Not figuratively, either. She literally smelled garbage and it made her gag. Gagging, in turn, woke the rest of her up with the spasms, and she blearily became aware of the world around her.

She was in an alley. There was garbage piled in the corners and overflowing a dumpster in front of her. Molds and slimes grew beneath the dumpster and in the cracks and crevices of the buildings. Those buildings were built of brick and looked old. She found herself laying half on a concrete sidewalk, and half in the single, narrow asphalt driving lane. Her heart exploded into hyperactivity when she looked down to see herself naked and covered in blood, fear gripping her. She scrambled backwards, pushing herself into a niche between another dumpster and several pipes running down the building behind her, pain screeching out of her back as she moved.

Her rapid breathing sent clouds of vapor out into the chill air, billowing away from her, announcing her presence to whatever unknown predators were out there. Lights flashed above, like someone in one of the windows was shining a flashlight around. She watched the beam move over the ground where she'd just lain before it vanished.

She tried to remember how she got there, but found only emptiness. She tried to remember earlier, and still found nothing. She tried to remember anything, but what came to her was her name… And two others.

Amanda. That was her name. Mike was…. Someone important to her. A friend, or maybe a lover. David was…. Also someone important, but in a different way. Someone she must find.

The tears came as the realization hit her that she was alone, lost and had no way home. She didn't even know where home was. Wet lines chilled her face as the tears ran down to drip off her chin.

She sat there and cried it out until calmness began to return. She began to think, to try and work it through, but a noise coming from further down the alley to her left startled her, a grim reminder that she was vulnerable. She pushed herself to her feet, using the pipes and dumpster as handholds. Her legs were unsteady as they took her weight, and she looked around for anything that could help her.

The first thing to catch her eye was a hose, coiled and resting on a mount next to a door in the building she was standing against. She checked the valve and found that it turned easily, releasing a stream of clear, cold water from the end of the hose. She stuck a finger in the end and used it to spray herself clean. The water burned like ice against her bare skin, but blood and dirt ran down her body in rivulets of reddish brown to pool on the concrete beneath her feet as she shivered. When she was clean, she sprayed the mess towards a storm drain, washing away the evidence. She wasn't sure why, but she felt it was important. She looked down and checked herself for injuries.

Her knuckles, elbows and knees were scraped, but the damage was superficial, except for one deeper gash on her left middle knuckle that slowly oozed blood. She also had two small burns on her chest, just below her clavicle. There was bruising around her hips, probably the edges of a large bruise across her back judging from the pain. She had more bruises scattered around on her ribs, tender splotches from ankles to chest, and on both arms.

Amanda cut off the flow of water and hung the hose back up, then walked over to the dumpster and dug through it. She found a shirt, an oversized men's t-shirt. It was filthy and stained with rotten food from the dumpster, and many sizes too big for her. She brought it back to the hose and sprayed and scrubbed at it with her hands, until she thought it might pass for clean in bad lighting.

She wrung the water out and pulled it over her head. The white fabric turned clear where it clung to her body, but it was better than nothing. It hung down almost to her knees, and was voluminous enough that any movement pulled it away from her skin. She took one step towards what seemed to be the mouth of the alley, but loud, raucous voices rose up from the streets and she froze.

Young males. Six. Intoxication likely. Threat assessment, 58%.

The voice spoke in her head, startling her. She jumped and spun, but there was no speaker to be seen. There was something ethereal about the voice. Like it didn't belong to a body. It was the voice of a ghost, an angel or demon. Or a computer, of course.

As she thought about a computer speaking in her head, the voice spoke again.

I am CompanionAssist Version 3. My visual communication module has been damaged and will not be functional for an unknown time. Audio communication is functioning normally.

A phrase came to her, rising from the void that was her memory. Brain-Computer Interface. Somehow, Amanda knew that some people had a computer in their brains, though she couldn't, for the life of her, recall ever getting one. She nonetheless very clearly had, at some point.

"What happened to me?" she whispered.

The voice remained silent. Amanda cursed and looked around for something that might trigger it again; to convince it to answer her question.

Unknown. Logs prior to Dec 26 2759 - 21:40:56 UTC are corrupted and inaccessible. System maintenance evaluations indicate significant head trauma and electric shock.

Amanda stopped and thought. Was the voice responding to her thoughts?

I am responding to any thoughts directed at me.

Amanda turned back and scurried deeper into the alley as the voices grew louder and shadows appeared on the street at the mouth. She ducked back behind the dumpster that she had woken up against.

She tried to recall anything she might know and not be aware of, hoping for a repeat of the brain-computer interface tidbit. But the not-being-aware-of-it part made the task exceedingly difficult. She didn't get much; she vaguely recalled some psychology; making people feel good about themselves and convincing them of things they didn't already believe. As if to punish her for daring to dig up memories that were denied, she found some flashes of disturbing and painful sex acts that twisted her guts with apprehension. She stopped trying to remember then, afraid of what else she might find. She peeked out, carefully keeping her head in the shadows, and watched the group of young men walk past, talking loudly among themselves.

Hm. That was interesting. One of the men had stood out to her, a young fellow with a thick neck and significant scarring on his ears. She recognized that scarring as 'cauliflower', and knew that it came from engaging in competitive martial arts.

But how? How did she know that? Was it common knowledge, worked so deep into her brain that whatever had stripped the rest of her memories couldn't uproot it? Was it something near and dear to her, with roots too deep to pull cleanly out?

She checked her own ears. There were a few lumps and knots there, but nothing like the man's. She also found a pair of tiny stud earrings. So it wasn't personal knowledge, at least not in that way. She pulled one of the earrings out and looked at it, wondering where she'd gotten it and why.

Seely Jewelers, 1.3 Carat natural diamond studs, retail price: $1,799.99 per piece, or $3,499.99 for a set.

Huh. Amanda wondered how expensive that was.

Retail price is in the top 6% of all retail prices for advertised 1.3 carat diamond stud earrings.

This was going to take some getting used to.

She put the earring back, and lifted her shirt, again. She had more jewelry. Tiny silver barbells in each nipple, a banana-like barbel in the skin at the bottom of her naval. Another through her clitoral hood. She ran hands all over her body and found studs at the small of her back, one on either side of her spine, just a half-centimeter in diameter, same as the balls on the others and about ten centimeters apart. Another tiny spike protruded from just below her lower lip, and a barbell ran through her tongue. She swept fingers over her eyebrows and the bridge of her nose, but found nothing else.

She asked the voice in her head, and it told her that none of the other jewelry was worth more than a few dollars a piece. She lowered her scavenged shirt back and considered her next move. She could sell the earrings for money, but she'd need to scavenge for some better clothing before any jeweler who wouldn't immediately rip her off would even let her in the shop.

And she needed to get someplace warm, quickly. Her hands and feet were beginning to grow numb. She moved further into the alley. With luck, perhaps this alley would connect to one with some residential buildings on it, and she could steal some clothes hung out to dry.

She paced down the alley quietly on bare feet, breath steaming the air. She kept her head turning, eyes moving from one shadow to the next. Most of the lighting was incidental, coming from the cracks around blinds in the windows above her. The shadows were deep and dark, yet she could still…. Sense somehow, the shapes of things within them.

Amanda had gone no more than half a block when she stopped and froze. There, in front of her, where the alley she prowled met another, she could see steam rising in regular intervals. Someone was standing there. The amount of steam was much more than Amanda's own breath produced, and it occurred to her that they might be smoking. The buildings around her looked like the backs of businesses, and she realized that this might be just an employee, out on a smoke break.

She decided to approach whoever it was. She turned her face into a pitiful mask of fear and hunched her shoulders. It wasn't difficult, and she was already shivering, her teeth clattering together involuntarily.

She walked forward, the corner peeling back until she could see a large man with a shaved head, wearing a bulky jacket and blue jeans, leaning against one wall and puffing on an electronic cigar.

"Exc-excuse m-m-me, can-n y-you help m-m-me?, p-p-p-p-please?" she chattered as she came within the man's view. The man started as she spoke and pushed himself off the wall.

"Where the fuck did you come from?" he demanded. Amanda noted that he had a thick accent that felt familiar. She couldn't name it, but she somehow knew that it was local.

"I d-d-don't know… I j-just w-w-woke up in the alley… Please, I'm sc-sc-scared…" More tears poured from her eyes. Her panic and fear was returning at the prospect of salvation, like it was trying to drag her back down with it.

"The fuck? What do you mean, you just woke up? Like you got knocked out?"

He eyed her up and down, his eyes lingering on her legs just below the hem of the overly large shirt. An uneasy feeling began to stir in her gut, warring with a sense of baleful familiarity.

"I c-c-can't remb-b-b-ber anything, please!"

"Calm down, calm down," he said, taking a step towards her. Alarms went off in her head. Amanda flinched back instinctively. That terrible sense of familiarity filled her. She knew this scene, knew what it meant. It meant danger, pain and more fear. The man continued forward, closing the distance with long legs. "Your shirt's soaking wet," he said, "You should get out of it before you catch pneumonia."

He darted a hand out and grabbed the hem, pulling up to expose her to his view. She jerked back harder, but the man's grip on her shirt didn't waver and the movement tripped her up. She fell backwards, her weight finally pulling the shirt from the man's grasp as she landed on her back. Agony exploded from her lower back and made her spasm uncontrollably for a second. The loose, wet cloth of her shirt flew up and over her face in the process. She grabbed at it frantically, trying to get it off of her head so she could see, and she heard the man's voice, laughing. "Hey hey! Nice!"

Hands seized her ankles and yanked backwards. Amanda finally clawed the fabric off her face to see the man on his knees between her legs, fumbling at his belt, his head turning from side to side for witnesses to the rape he intended to commit. The image of him kneeling there filled her with a sense of deja vu. She had seen this before. She had been here before. She knew what to do, if only she could remember...

Her attempts to remember drew a blank, and fear won out over instincts. She opened her mouth to scream, and as she did, something abruptly clicked in her head.

The fear and panic vanished in an instant, replaced by a cool, calm certainty. She knew what to do. The man was a threat, and threats are to be eliminated.

Amanda snapped her mouth shut. She drew back a foot and then shot it forward into the man's face, feeling the bones of his nose crunch beneath her heel. As he shouted in pain and reeled back, she raised both legs up and over her head, rolling backwards to a crouch.

"You fucking bitch!" the man shouted, letting go of his nose and lurching back forward, grabbing at her arms. She let him get a grip, then snapped her head forward into his, producing another, wetter crack. He fell backwards with another cry and she swarmed on top of him, mounting his chest and throwing a flurry of punches.

The man flailed and tried to throw her off, but she expertly adjusted her weight and the position of her legs to keep her mount, continuing to rain down blows through his meager defenses. After a few moments, he stopped struggling. After a few more moments, the hard, strange angles of his skull had been reduced to a chunky, squishy mess of blood and tissue. After a few more moments, his chest ceased rising and falling. She continued to slam her fists down.

Eventually, Amanda stood and reeled backwards. Something clicked again.

The horror of what she'd just done swept over her and she bent in half and hurled vomit onto the ground. The smell hit her and she vomited more, dropping to her knees. She quickly found herself dry heaving over a pile of stinking, steaming vomit and rolled away from it, sitting with her back to one wall and staring at the dead body.

Her mind went blank, and she sat there, thinking of nothing for a long moment.

After a while, something began to gnaw at her. She watched the large puddle of blood below his head elongate out and run down the alley, away from him for several minutes before it clicked.

His clothes were still clean. She moved forward to the body. Well, they weren't entirely clean. There was blood on his jacket, tiny droplets having splattered it from her assault. She wiped at them, but her bloody fingers succeeded only in smearing more blood on it. She looked about and saw another hose, next to the door the man had been standing next to.

She washed her hands off, then tried again. The jacket was waterproof, and the blood wiped away easily this time. She cleaned it as best she could and then stripped him out of it. She threw the jacket over her shoulders and pushed her arms into the sleeves. She felt it squirm and adjust itself to fit her. Threads drew tighter throughout it, shortening the sleeves and the hem, tightening the stomach, relaxing the chest ever so slightly. She moved her arms experimentally, and found that her wet undershirt was uncomfortable. So she stripped off the jacket and shirt, and then put the jacket back on and buttoned it up. That was much better.

She looked back at the corpse. She didn't know where her sudden assault had come from, and she was too scared to ponder the question right now. She finished undoing the man's belt, then took off his shoes and his pants, exposing a dirty pair of boxers. Amanda wrinkled her nose at the smell, but squirmed into the pants anyways. The waist was too big, and they weren't smart garments like the jacket, so she had to bunch it up by cinching the belt tightly around her waist.

She folded up the legs until they were a good length for her, ripped her scavenged shirt in half and used it to bind her feet up into thick bundles of cloth. She pulled the man's large boots on over this, and wiggled her toes experimentally. It wasn't ideal, but it would work.

She stood and checked her pockets, jacket and pants. She found a large wad of crumpled red bills and counted them out. $423.

There was nothing else but a pocket knife, in one of the jacket pockets. She inspected it.

`Public domain design, 1085 steel blade, plastic handle, stainless steel pins. Retail value, approximately $7.`

She tested the edge. It was dull as a spoon, and nicked in a few places. It was a cheap knife, mostly worthless, but possibly useful for self-defense. Amanda realized that's probably what the man had it for, though it hadn't done him any good in the end.

She turned away, back the way she'd come, towards the street. With reasonable clothes, she could walk into a jewelry store or pawn shop, assuming one was open at this time. Even if they were all closed, she felt less vulnerable now. She moved with a slouched, rolling gait with which she associated soldiers and martial artists. She didn't know if her feelings about it were accurate, but it made her feel better, so she kept it up. After a few moments, she walked out onto the street and looked both ways. To her right, the street ran a long, straight path, the street lights ending about halfway to the horizon, though she could see the break in the buildings that indicated that the street continued past it.

To her left, she saw brightly colored lights. That way was downtown. That's where the businesses would all be. That's also where the homeless would go, letting the heat of the city help stave off the cold. At best, she could find a place to sell her earrings for enough money to have some cash to help her figure out who she was and how she got here. At worst, she could find a homeless camp where the other residents would be loath to cause a scene, lest they draw down the cops on themselves.

She looked back to her right. Something inside of her told her that was the way to go, that it was the way she'd been heading before whatever happened that left her unconscious, naked in that alley. She tried so hard to remember what it was, but nothing came to her. Eventually, with a sigh, she rationalized that her move to downtown would be temporary. As soon as she had some money, she could return and head down the long, straight road out of the city.

She turned left and walked.

Alive

Amanda counted out two hundred and seventeen of her stolen dollars and handed them to the clerk. The clerk looked at the cash -an ancient tradition kept alive mostly by criminals and panhandlers- and made a face, but took it. Businesses were required by law to keep cash on hand for transactions under $10,000, at least, according to the small-print sign next to the register. The young woman carefully placed the bills into the tender box and uncertainly counted out sixty eight cents in change before handing it over, along with Amanda's receipt.

Amanda smiled, despite the chilly reception. "Thank you. Now, do you have a bathroom I could use?"

The clerk sighed deeply. Amanda didn't really blame her. She was dressed like a homeless person or a drug addict, and both groups tended to leave messes in public bathrooms, which the clerk would probably have to clean up. Fortunately for her, Amanda only wanted to use the sink and toilet, and to change into her new outfit. The clerk hitched a thumb over her shoulder and deadpanned "All the way back, on the left."

Amanda walked back with her bag and found the little girl's room. She stripped off her dirty, stolen clothes and sat down on the toilet to relieve herself. When she was done, she used the sink and the provided liquid soap and some paper towels to bathe herself. She washed away the stink of sweat and blood and the alley where she had found herself.

When she was done, she pulled on her new panties and bra, then gave her still-moist torso a spritz with the tiny sampler bottle of perfume she'd gotten from a basket of free samples. The name -Desert Rose- had sounded familiar, though she didn't know where she knew it from. She checked the level in the bottle when she was done, and saw that she'd used almost all of it. With a shrug, she emptied the bottle on herself, then wiped off the excess with a paper towel. At least the bathroom would smell nice when she was done.

She pulled out the cheap designer jeans she'd picked out and pulled them on. They settled and adjusted themselves the way they were programmed to, by pulling taut all around her thighs and hips and butt. Next came a simple white cotton undershirt, which she tucked into the pants. A long-sleeve, men's shirt went on over that, and she used the stick of deodorant she'd picked up from a pharmacy an hour ago before tucking it in. Checking herself out in the mirror, she unbuttoned the top few buttons of the overshirt. There, that looked right.

The boots were stylish and sleek, with plenty of faux straps and buckles, so she slipped them on over her jeans after pulling on a pair of socks. They looked rough and tough, but she doubted they would stand up to much abuse, given where she'd bought them. Hopefully, she wouldn't abuse them too much.

Finally, she threw her new sweater on. It was not smart fabric, but a simple gray hoodie that would be equally at place in a dive bar or a country club. Good. She looked more like a middle-class housewife, and less like an amnesiac who'd traded a handjob to a homeless man for a chance to sleep snuggled up with him in a warm and defensible looking spot underneath an overpass, five blocks from here.

There was still something missing, though… She examined herself for a few moments before the realization struck. Makeup.

No self-respecting middle-class housewife would be out on the town without makeup, not even to run errands. She stuffed her old clothes into the bag after removing the little clutch purse and attaching the thin shoulder strap to it. She put her empty perfume bottle, her cheap, dull knife, her remaining cash, her stick of deodorant and the leftover socks and panties from the plastic-wrapped packages in which she'd bought them in the purse, then flung it over her shoulder, lifted the bag and walked out.

As she passed the clerk, she paused. "Where can I get some affordable makeup around here? The pharmacy down on Clancy Street didn't have any."

The clerk eyed her suspiciously before answering. "The pharmacies downtown aren't allowed to sell makeup, just drugs and candy and hygiene stuff. There's a Cindy's Boutique two blocks down, left out the door. They're not too expensive." Amanda smiled and thanked the girl, then turned to leave.

"You didn't leave a mess in the bathroom, did you?" the clerk called out. Amanda stopped and looked over her shoulder, her annoyance with the rude clerk finally boiling over.

"You know, old needles. Shit on the walls."

Amanda's eyes narrowed. She'd been nothing but polite to this girl, yet met nothing but suspicion and judgment in response. "Nothing but a couple splashes of menstrual blood and some old tar heroin baggies, dear," she said with a sweet smile.

She left to the sound of the clerk groaning as she walked back to survey the damage.

Amanda walked the two blocks to where the makeup, hair and faux-jewelry chain had their nearest franchise and then walked in. She browsed the selection for a moment as the cute woman behind the register watched her with a pained expression. Amanda didn't give the look too much thought, though. The clerk at the fashion store had been warmer and more receptive than the man at the pharmacy and convenience store had been. He'd only given her about thirty seconds to browse before demanding she pay and leave.

Eventually, she chose eyeliner and a dark red eyeshadow. The hair she'd seen in the mirror for the first time this morning was black, with blood red stripes in it, and she figured a middle-class housewife would care about things like matching her makeup to her hair. She'd picked her clothing out with the same thought in mind, electing for black jeans with a few artful (and titillating) rips at the base of the butt and around her knees and a rich, maroon shirt.

She added a dark red lipstick to her haul and paused to examine her face in one of the many mirrors. She didn't think she'd need foundation. Her skin was smooth and unblemished.

She wondered if she was a model, or maybe a gold digger. Whatever her life had been like, she'd clearly cared for her appearance. Maybe she was a high-priced call-girl, she thought, remembering how easily she'd agreed to get the homeless man off last night in exchange for a place to sleep.

Whatever. She planned to find out soon enough. She just needed money for that, and in order to get money, she had to look respectable. She brought her haul up to the front, where the clerk seemed to have forgotten the odd look she'd given Amanda just a moment ago. She favored her with a bright smile and announced "I love your hair!"

Amanda smiled back, "Thank you," she said, placing her selection on the counter.

"I've tried to do that with my hair," the clerk said as she scanned the items, "but with curls, it's *really* hard to get the stripes to stay clumped together. I have to put product in, and then it gets all stiff… Ugh. It's just not worth it."

Amanda eyed the clerk for a moment. She was a short, curvaceous thing with hair curly enough to look like ringlets. It was done up in a bun on top, with the sides left free to cascade down to her shoulders. She had a pretty face and an open, enthusiastic smile.

"I think you're doing a lovely job with your hair already," Amanda said with a smile, relieved to be having an easier time than at the last shop. "You've got kind of a Greek goddess thing going, very sexy."

The woman blushed and glanced down at Amanda's hands, then back up to meet her eyes. "Thank you," she said. "It's just how my hair naturally sits. I'm always a little self conscious about it."

The clerk, whose name-tag read "Sasha," bit her lower lip and eyed Amanda silently for a second, slowly putting her purchases into a small bag. Amanda wondered if she was being flirted with.

Hormonal response is consistent with sexual arousal. Body language is inconclusive, but based on generalized criteria, there is a high likelihood of sexual interest.

Amanda blinked. She hadn't heard the voice since she ran out of the alley last night, and she'd almost forgotten about it. She recalled what it had said about visual communication and wondered how that was going.

Visual communication module will be restored to adequate functionality in two to four hours.

Amanda gave the clerk a good once-over with her eyes and smiled a small, hungry smile at her. It wasn't deliberate; she found the woman quite attractive. There was something about her that just invited Amanda's interest.

"I'm Amanda," she said, holding out a hand. Sasha took it in one of hers, and Amanda felt a slight tremble, as if the interaction were scaring her. "Sasha," she said, smiling coyly. She held on to

Amanda's hand, her face shifting through a couple of microexpressions.

Nervous much? Amanda thought. Eventually, the moment drew out a little too long.

"My total?" she asked.

"Would yo- Oh, yes, I'm so sorry… Your total is thirteen sixty eight."

Amanda reached into her purse and counted out exact change. The clerk blinked at the cash, but gamely opened the tender and threw it in, then ripped off the receipt and used a pen she retrieved from her own ample cleavage to write something on it before handing it over along with the bag.

Amanda took it and gave the woman another look up and down. Out of no-where, the thought came to her that Mike would find her appealing.

There was that name again. Amanda tried to recall more, but nothing came, except the same vague sense that Mike was important to her. She wondered again what had happened.

Unknown. Logs prior to Dec 26 2759 - 21:40:56 UTC are corrupted and inaccessible. System maintenance evaluations indicate significant head trauma and electric shock.

She sighed. *I wasn't asking you*, she thought at the stupid computer, turning and walking out. She glanced down at the receipt and recognized that the woman had written "Sasha - 48-562-09-6-24831" on it. Her name and phone number. She had *definitely* been flirting. The pained look when Amanda had first walked in must have just been an odd reaction to seeing an attractive person.

Amanda walked a half a block, then paused to sit at a little bench tucked into an alcove. The eyeshadow came in a little compact, so she took it out and used the tiny mirror to apply the makeup to her face. Her hands moved with practiced ease, and the whole process took less than a minute.

There, finally. She held the compact at arm's length and examined herself. She fully looked the part, now. When she walked into a jeweler's shop to sell her earrings, the proprietor wouldn't immediately peg her as a thief, and thus in a position to be taken advantage of.

She walked for a while through the crowds. Bots and pedestrians alike filled the sidewalks, talking on their phones or to their companions, or just marching determinedly to their destinations. Ignoring the bots, there were two clear groups. One group was dressed nicely, like Amanda in smart garment or tailored clothing. They were stylish and well-manicured, and looked happy, for the most part. The other group wore loose-fitting, stained clothing with holes and patches. They outnumbered the first group by about ten to one, and on balance, looked neutral. Many seemed distraught, and she overheard more than one crying on the phone to someone.

The faces of the second group almost all had a characteristic squint to them. Amanda wondered what it meant.

Stress.

She focused her thoughts on the voice and tried to get it to elaborate.

The violent crime rate in the People's Republic of Arthesia is the fifth highest in the galaxy, with 242 homicides per 100,000 citizens every year. The average citizen's odds of being the victim of a violent crime is 42 percent over the course of their lifetime if perpetrators are limited to persons unknown to the victim, and 89.97 percent if perpetrators known to the victim are included. 17 percent of citizens surveyed admit to having connections to organized crime, and estimates of actual participation in organized crime range from 23 to 38 percent.

In addition, 78 percent of citizens live below the poverty line. The combination of high crime and poverty, along with a low unemployment rate has been cited in numerous studies finding that citizens of the People's Republic of Arthesia to be among the most stressed civilian population in the galaxy.

Amanda reflected on that for a moment. The homeless camps were certainly busy places. She had passed through two before finding one she liked the looks of, and even that one had several dozen residents. The first one she encountered was a miniature city of its own; with homemade signs scrawled on cardplastic sheets, stuck up over cardplastic stores, tucked in between countless cardplastic hovels.

And that was with record low unemployment, if the computer in her brain was to be believed. She signed, and wondered if it would be possible to get away from this awful country when she got her memories back.

She looked around for jewelers. She wanted a small shop with a nice front, the kind of place where a woman such as the one she appeared to be would go. Not too high-brow to purchase jewelry for cash, but not so shady that thieves would try to fence their stolen goods there.

It took several hours, during which her stomach began to rumble with increasing urgency. She promised herself she would find some food as soon as she got her money. She found a couple of places, but rejected each one. She was beginning to consider taking a break to eat when she finally found the perfect shop.

It was a small one, nestled in between a large and expensive fashion boutique and an equally expensive-looking phone store. She paused on her way in to glance at the phones, wondering if she should buy one.

You can place phone calls or access the internet using your CompanionAssist.

Huh. So she didn't need one. Well, good to know. Her mind drifted to the phone number on her receipt, but she shook her head. There were more important things to consider.

She stepped into the shop. The sign above the door had called it Marcus Creations. As she did, a small bell attached to the top of the door rang, alerting an older, distinguished looking gentleman who was working on something behind the counter. He flipped up his magnifying glasses and regarded her.

"Do you have an escort, miss, or are you here by yourself?" he asked.

"An escort?" Amanda responded. She wasn't sure what he meant.

"Yes, your owner."

Amanda blinked in surprise and indignation. "I don't have an owner! I came here to sell some old jewelry, but if you're just going to be an asshole, I can go somewhere else…"

The man stood and hurried around the counter. "I'm very sorry, miss. You look like one of the Viridian Seven series Companions, but it was entirely my mistake. You are very clearly a well-to-do young lady, and I offer my unreserved apologies for the mistake. It will not happen again, I promise. Will you forgive me?"

The man, who must be Marcus, bowed slightly in apology, and Amanda gritted her teeth and reminded herself why she was here. "Okay, you're forgiven."

The man smiled at her and walked back behind the counter. "Very well. You said something about selling some jewelry?"

Amanda walked forward, taking the earrings out of her purse and placing them on a black felt pad on the glass countertop. "Yes, these."

Marcus picked one up and examined it briefly. "I don't have my monocle, but are these from Chan Jewels, over in Baipan?"

"Um," Amanda said, "I think they're Seeley?"

The man set the earring back down and retrieved a monocle. "I hope not," he said, "I don't have much use for Seeley work. Mass manufactured, the lot of it. There's no love in it. But Chan... Well, Debra used to work for Seeley, as a designer. After they let her go -for no good reasons, she says- she made a tradition of remaking every design they put out, only doing it with much better craftsmanship. Sort of a 'look what you're missing out on' statement, I think."

Marcus put the monocle in his eye and picked the earring back up. He examined it, then set it down and checked the next one. "Aha, yes, this is definitely one of Debra's pieces. I can understand why you thought it might be a Seeley, but this craftsmanship is well beyond what their bots can do."

He placed the earring back down and removed his monocle. "So how much were you looking to get for it?"

Amanda panicked for a second. The proprietor had implied that they were worth more than she'd expected, but she didn't know how much more. She reached out to the voice in her head.

There is insufficient data about sales of Chan Jewels merchandise to establish a firm retail value. Calculations based on three advertised prices versus comparable items from Seeley Jewelers suggests a value of $7000 plus or minus $1300.

"Um, uh..." She stammered to stall for time as she crunched the numbers the voice had given her. "Let's say, seventy five hundred?"

The gentleman shook his head. "You might be able to get that price in a private sale, but I don't think I could part with more than five thousand for them."

Pupillary activity and stress hormones indicate eagerness. 80% possibility that this is a lowball offer in preparation for a negotiated agreement.

Amanda cocked her head to the side and smiled slightly at the man, as if she found him amusing. "I already know I could get that much because my cousin offered me as much. But I don't like my cousin, so maybe I could go down to seven thousand."

Marcus rubbed the bridge of his nose and resumed his seat. He sighed. "I could do fifty seven fifty, if you like."

"Sixty six hundred," Amanda countered.

"Sixty *two* hundred," the man responded immediately, "And I'm afraid that's my final offer. If you sold them privately, that would be to someone who would wear them. I, on the other hand, would be obliged to resell them to pay my bills, and I can't pay my bills if I don't make any profit off the sale."

Amanda considered it. It was almost double what she'd originally hoped for. It really wasn't a difficult choice, but now that it was down to the actual sale, she found herself strangely reluctant.

"Tell me the truth," she said, "Would Debra Chan offer me a refund for them, if I told her I was returning them because the man who bought them for me cheated on me?"

Marcus laughed. "Possibly," he said, "But I wouldn't get my hopes up. Debra is a hard woman, with not a lot of sympathy to spare."

"Still," Amanda said, "I think I'll give it a shot. If she says no, I'll bring them back here and sell them to you for, let's say, six thousand, sound fair?"

The jeweler nodded. "Fair enough. Do you remember how to get there?"

"Um, now that you mention it, no. I don't think I've ever been. The earrings were a gift."

The man opened a drawer and fished around a bit, then came back with a plastic business card. It said "Chan Jewels: Handmade, only the finest craftsmanship sold" and had a phone number, a website and an address on it.

He handed the card over and Amanda took it. "Thank you," she said, "You've been very helpful. I'll stop by and let you know what happened, either way."

"Apologies again for my mistake, earlier. When Debra turns you down, I'll be here," the man said distractedly, his attention already returning to the engagement ring she could now see he was working on.

She left, and looked down at the card in her hand. She thought at the voice, willing it to give her directions.

`Turn right. Proceed for 2.3 kilometers.`

Amanda smiled, feeling as if she was finally getting the hang of dealing with the voice. She walked down the sidewalk, avoiding the shadier-looking characters and anyone who seemed to be angry. There were a lot of such people.

A couple blocks away from the jewelry shop, she found a sign above a narrow alley that said "Noodle Bar" so she turned in to find a stand selling plastic bowls of noodles and cans of beer and soda. She ordered two bowls of noodles and stood leaning against a wall to eat them. When she was done, she continued, following the voice's directions into a nicer part of the downtown area, though she could see dirty streets and people through the alleys. Like many nicer commercial areas, this one was surrounded by slums.

She finally found the place, and was relieved to see that it was still open, as the day was getting late. She walked in to find a very well appointed store. It was much less cluttered than the last place, and all of the surfaces she could see were either glass or white marble with gold veins.

"Hello?" she called, not seeing anyone.

A moment later, a door behind the longest counter opened to reveal a handsome woman dressed in an immaculate, formal pants suit. Metallic dust on her hands and cuffs glittered in the bright lights as the woman stopped behind the counter and gave her a good once over, her expression a tight mask of matronly disapproval. Debra Chan, Amanda presumed.

"Good evening, my dear. How are you? And how is Mike?" she asked.

Amanda started. "You know Mike?" she asked, breathlessly. Perhaps the journey back to her life would be quicker than she thought.

"Better than I care to, and I hasten to add that you should not take that to suggest that I know him well."

"Do you know where he is?"

The woman's look softened a tiny bit. "I'm afraid I haven't a clue, dearest. Is that why you're here? Are you searching for him?"

Amanda's mind whirled with this new information. She pondered what to do. Should she explain her situation and ask for the woman's help? After the man she encountered in the alley, she wasn't sure she wanted to do that. But this woman was far less likely to turn into an attempted rapist, so…

Debra knew Mike. Hell, the woman knew Amanda, even if only from the one time. Amanda thought it over, and decided to roll the dice. She'd come here planning to feed the woman a sob story in any event, it was probably best to give her the truthful sob story.

She approached the counter and let the woman see the hope and fear on her face.

"I've lost my memory. Almost all of it. All I can remember are a few names, my own, Mike, someone named David… I woke up last night in an alley off Leung Highway, a couple kilometers east of downtown. I was naked and covered in blood, and I couldn't remember anything. I came here to sell my earrings, earrings that I think Mike bought for me, from you, so I could get the money to go to the hospital. If you know me, if you know Mike, please tell me what you know. Anything would help, please."

Her voice had cracked during her entreaty, and her eyes filled with tears. The woman looked dispassionately back at her all through her plea, then drew in a deep breath at the end. Amanda thought she saw something click. When Debra spoke again, her voice was much softer.

"Oh, dear. I'm sorry, but I don't really know Mike, he was just a street kid who hung out around here. Ran with some older boys for a long time. Petty crime and causing trouble was all I really knew him for. I figured him for a lost cause, same as most of the other street rats, but then one day, a couple weeks ago, he showed up here with you. He told me it was your birthday, and he wanted to get you a present. I, of course, told him that he couldn't afford anything I sold, but he pulled out a credit card with his name on it. He told me he had gained employment as a 'security consultant' and that he was making 'the big bucks', in his own words. You browsed around for a bit and picked out a pair of earrings. I rang you up, Mike paid with his new card, and I haven't seen either one of you since, until you walked in just now."

"What was I wearing?" Amanda asked. It sounded like a silly question the moment she asked it, but her intent was to grill the woman for every detail she could.

"A rather revealing skirt and an even more revealing top." Amanda could hear the disapproval in her voice. "You looked like a street walker, to be frank. I figured you for some working girl Mike was trying to show off for, though you are quite the fair bit better looking than most."

"And Mike?"

"Mike was dressed in his usual manner. Baggy shorts, baggy shirt, that stupid blue baseball cap he loved so much, turned sideways as usual."

"Did either of us say anything unusual? Did we talk about home, or our families, or anything like that?"

"I… Listen, dear, I don't really remember. If you want…" the woman sighed, as if what she was about to say went against her better judgment, "If you want, you can come in the back with me and look at the security footage. I archive everything, so I've still got it."

Amanda smiled. "Please? That would be so helpful, ma'am, you have no idea."

"Come on," Debra beckoned her around the counter, and then added under her breath, "You poor thing…"

Amanda followed her through the same door she'd emerged from, down a narrow hallway and into a tiny office with a single holomonitor on the small desk. A keyboard and a floating mouse sat idle.

"Let's see," the woman said, sitting down at the desk. Amanda had to press herself into the wall to let her pass, but when she tucked her legs under the desk, a bit more room opened up. The older woman seized the mouse and gave it a shake, and the monitor sprung to life, showing an interface for a security camera network.

"This would have been December 8th, because the 9th was when I got that delivery of silver stock..." She worked the keyboard and mouse and quickly had a three dimensional recreation of the inside of her shop up on the monitor.

"Flip those lights off, hun. These holos are much easier to see in the dark."

Amanda complied and with the lights off, the holo was indeed much easier to see. It looked almost solid, like a miniature model. As she watched, a few people walked in and browsed around at high speeds, with Debra moving in and out of the back door regularly. After a few moments, a couple walked in. "That's it!" Amanda shouted.

Debra rewound slightly, then played it again, at normal speed. A few clicks turned on the sound. A digital chime went off as Mike opened the door and held it for her. A wave of emotions washed over her as she peered closely at his holographic face. Warmth. Hope. Amanda zones out for a second, just riding the wave. She broke free when she saw a woman step through the door.

Debra was right, Amanda looked like a street whore. She wore a garish pink shade of lipstick, a miniskirt that exposed the bottoms of her ass cheeks and a top that was probably half of a two-piece bikini. She moved with a sauntering grace, swaying her hips with every step.

Mike said something she couldn't quite make out and she saw herself laugh, as if it were the funniest thing in the world. He put an arm around her waist and pulled her in tight to him, then kissed her. She kissed back, eagerly, and then the rear door opened and Debra came out.

"Can you turn the volume up?" The older woman obliged, and Amanda could finally make out what was said.

"Mike, you had better not have any ideas of causing trouble to impress your lady friend."

Mike looked affronted and put a hand to his chest. "Lady, I'm just here to buy my girl a birthday present. No need to get all personal and shit."

"Uh huh," the holo-Debra responded, "As if you could afford anything I sell. Go on, shoo. If you want to disappoint that poor girl, you could show her what you've got in those baggy pants of yours."

"Ugh, ruuuuude," the holo-Amanda said.

"Chill out, Miss Chan, I'm good for it. Look." Mike reached into one drooping pocket and pulled out a wallet, which he flipped open and pulled a card from. He stepped up and laid it on the counter. "Finantech Black, boom. No spending limit."

"Who did you steal this from?" The holo-Debra picked up the card and examined it.

"Jesus, lady, give me a little credit. Only an idiot would come in here with a stolen card to try and buy jewelry. Look at the name."

"Mike Flannigan. How the fuck did you pull that off?"

"I got a new gig. Security consultant for a big government contract project. Three years of steady work and a paycheck big enough that I can retire when it's done. Plus an expense account I was told wouldn't ever be looked at by anyone but my boss. And my boss don't give a shit what I do with the Junta's money, isn't that right, baby?" He looked over at Amanda who smirked and flashed him a wink.

"It's not a Junta anymore, young man. It is currently a 'provisional government'. Le Roi est mort, vive le Roi."

"I don't fucking know anyone named Roy, I just know I got me a job that pays. So my girl here is gonna pick out whatever she wants for her birthday."

Amanda watched herself browse the shop silently for a while. When the holo-her spotted the earrings, she immediately asked for them. As holo-Debra retrieved them, Mike frowned. "They seem a little... I dunno. Plain, I guess. Don't you want something nicer?"

"They're classy, you brute," holo-Amanda replied, "I like classy."

"Okay," Mike said, "We can do classy. It's all up to you, babe."

Holo-Amanda tried them on, checking out her reflection in a small mirror that holo-Debra held up for her. "I like them. This is what I want."

"Then that's what you get."

Holo-Debra walked over to the register, where Mike's card was still sitting on the counter. She tapped the card to the machine, grabbed the receipt, and held them both out. Mike retrieved them while holo-Amanda checked herself out in the mirror. She smiled.

There was no more conversation after that. The holo-couple left and turned left out the door, walking out of view on the sidewalk.

Debra turned off the projector and Amanda turned the lights back on.

"That's it, hun. That's the last time I saw either of you. I'm sorry, I don't know anything that might help you out. Debra paused, then added "Except…"

Amanda perked up. "Yes?"

"Mike used to hang out with this fellow, Ming. Ming Porter. I think they lived together for a while, in one of the flophouses those fellows pool their money for. I don't know where that was, but I know that Ming has been staying with my cousin's daughter in an in-law suite on her parent's property, over in Manyan province."

"Do you think he might know where Mike is?"

Debra paused, staring at Amanda thoughtfully for a moment. She spoke slowly.

"He might. I can give you their address, but you have to promise me you'll go to the in-law suite, and avoid the rest of the property. They don't like trespassers, and they're none to gentle with them, if you know what I mean."

Amanda did not, in fact, know what the older woman meant, but she nodded as if she did. It would be easy enough to avoid idle exploration. She had every intention of going straight to Ming.

"Let's have your phone, dear." Debra held out a hand.

Amanda stared at the hand for a moment, her mind caught up in the possibilities of finding her past, not understanding the request. When the words registered, she exclaimed. "I don't have one."

"What? Hun, you can't be running around with no phone! If a cop scans you or you try to pass through a checkpoint, you'll be arrested!"

Amanda blinked in confusion. She had passed through a checkpoint to get here. The cops at the stop had waved their phones at her, checked them, and then waved her on. She only realized then that they had scanned her for something electronic. She'd thought the scan was only for weapons, and had left the pocket knife in a garbage can a block before the checkpoint.

So how had she gotten through?

Your CompanionAssist contains your government identification number.

Well, okay then. Amanda already knew she could use it for navigation, and it had said she could place phone calls and use the internet with it. She supposed that was her phone.

"I, uh. I have a BCI. In my head."

Debra balked and gave Amanda a suspicious appraisal. "What the fuck you need that for?" Her accent suddenly sounded different, more like Mike's had been on the holo. It was a street accent. Amanda remembered what Marcus had said at the other jewelry shop; that Debra had once worked for the big name jeweler. She wasn't sure why she felt like that made sense, but it did.

Seeley Jewelers has a clause in its charter that requires it to hire an unknown percentage of its creative talent from disadvantaged families and build production plants in financially struggling regions.

Well, that was one minor mystery solved. Now onto the next.

"I, uh… I don't know. I don't remember."

"Uh huh. Girl, I'm starting to wonder what is up with you. You come to me with this story about losing your memory that's straight out of the movies. You're looking for Mike, a kid who was a street rat heading for an early grave, who somehow got his hands on a legit black card with no spending limit. You've got bruised and banged up knuckles that I damn well know come from throwing bones, and you've gone from looking and talking and acting like a working girl to looking and talking and acting like this well-off… Whatever you are. And now you're telling me you have this military-grade hardware in your head?"

Amanda stared at her. She didn't know what to say, what would alleviate this woman's concerns. The change in mannerisms had thrown her off, even with the explanation provided by the voice.

Debra leaned forward, and spoke in a conspiratorial whisper.

"Are you a fucking spy?"

"No!" Amanda exclaimed. "No, I'm… I don't think I am! Please, listen, I don't know a lot, but I know that Mike was someone important. Not just, like, to my job, but to *me*. The thought of finding him makes me happy, I just know he's someone I care about, who cares about me. I need to find him, because if he cares about me, then he has to know about me, too! He can help me remember!"

"Uh huh," Debra leaned back, still eyeing Amanda critically.

"Who was the other fella?"

"What?" Amanda asked.

"The other fella! You said you remembered three names. Your own, Mike, and, what was it, Dave?"

"Oh, yes, uh, David. He's… He's important too, but in the other way. Like it's my job to find him."

"So, you're hunting a man."

"No!" Amanda objected. This wasn't right! She wasn't a secret agent or some assassin, she was… Something…. Something else. She could *feel* it. She remembered the way she'd vomited after seeing what she had done to the man in the alley, and she clung to that feeling. She did her best to ignore the little voice that asked her *how* she had managed to do such things to that man as tears of frustration welled in her eyes.

Something in her words or her body language must have made an impact, because Debra's look softened slowly, and after a moment she leaned forward and wrapped her arms around Amanda's waist. Amanda melted as soon as she felt the hug. It was as if the air around her had been increasing in pressure ever since she woke up last night, and it suddenly relaxed. She took a deep breath, and smelled perfume and metal coming off of Debra.

"Oh, don't cry, honey. I believe you. It's going to be alright. I'll tell you what. Give me a moment to close up, and then I'll drive you over to see Ming yourself. If he can't lead you to Mike, do you have a place to stay tonight?"

Amanda shook her head slightly. The hug felt good, and she was loath to break it. But Debra forced her hand, pulling back to study her face with concerned eyes. "No, I was going to try to return my earrings and hope I had enough to be seen at the hospital. I didn't…"

"Well, if you need it, you can stay with me. I have an unoccupied guest room at my home. We'll return your earrings tomorrow, after I open back up and you've had a chance to get your bearings, if you still need the money."

"Th-thank you," Amanda said in a small voice. She felt overwhelmed by this larger-than-life woman and her grand gestures and ever-changing personality.

"Okay, you wait here, and I'll close up. I'll just be a moment." Debra stood and squeezed past her, and then vanished back down the hall. A moment later, the holo lit up again, and Amanda glanced at it.

It showed Debra walking out of the door behind the counter and standing at the register. She tapped a few spots on the control surface and waited while it did something. With nothing better to do, Amanda watched, idly wondering what all was entailed in closing the shop.

After a few seconds, the display on the register lit up again. Debra tapped it a few times, and then it went dark. She pulled out the tender and removed a few bills and then counted out some change, stuffing it all in a pocket of her jacket. When she was done, she returned the tender, pressed a button on the side of the register and then began walking around, pressing a button below each counter that caused the glass to turn an opaque, matte black.

As she opaqued the last counter, the door opened and Debra looked up.

"I'm sorry, sir, but I've just closed down the register for the night. I'm not able to make any more sales for the evening."

The man approached Debra, and Amanda squinted closer. There was something about him…

"I'm not here to buy anything, I just wanted to ask you some questions, if that's okay, ma'am."

The man stopped across from the counter Debra stood behind and clasped his hands behind his back. He kept his head slightly bowed in a respectful way, and patiently waited for an answer.

He was tall, and despite his polite manners, he looked like a thug. Muscular, veiny arms hung from broad shoulders, topped by a neck with a line of barbed wire tattooed around it that turned and ran up one side of his face to his hairline. His hair was cut short, not quite a military style, but not far off. He wore a simple olive-colored t-shirt and multi-pocketed pants, tucked into tightly strapped, high-mouthed hiking boots. His only concession to fashion over practicality was a thick silver chain that hung around his neck, and a matching bracelet around one wrist.

The way he carried himself, the way he moved bespoke a fighter, a man who knew how to throw his fists. Amanda glanced at his ears, and even in the tiny model, she could see little distortions of cauliflowering. It wasn't much, but given his vibe, Amanda suspected that it was more that he was better at not getting hit, than that he might be inexperienced in a fight.

The sense of familiarity grew stronger. Amanda pushed off the wall and walked down the hall towards the store to get a better look at him, hearing his voice first fading from her rear, and then increasing in volume from her front.

"Have you seen this man any time in the past few weeks?"

Amanda walked through the door. The man's eyes flicked instantly to her as soon as she stepped through. As she met them with her own gaze, familiarity gave way to sudden certainty.

"David?" she asked.

The man frowned. "I'm sorry?"

"Is that your name," Amanda asked, "David?"

"No," the man responded smoothly. "My name's cristobol Alvares. You can call me Chris."

His face belied his words. Amanda had seen the shock flash through his eyes for just the barest fraction of a second when she said his name. Amanda could hear the practiced ease with which he gave a different name. He was a liar of one sort or another, and, she suspected, a damned good one. But not quite as good as she, it seemed.

Debra looked back and forth between them. "Dear, is there-"

She never got to finish the sentence. Her jacket puffed out suddenly and a small hole appeared in it. At the same instant, the large picture window that displayed her wares to the street shattered, and something stung Amanda's cheek.

Debra looked down at her chest. "What?" she asked, and then blood began welling from the hole, soaking the cloth in an expanding circle around it. Debra stumbled and dropped to one knee.

"Shit!" Chris/David shouted, spinning to face the shattered window and holding up something he'd snatched from the back of his belt. A wide metal disc flowed into shape between him and the window, just in time for a bullet to smack into it with a meaty, metallic clang.

Amanda gasped in surprise and rushed forward to Debra. She slid around behind her, getting her arms under the older woman's and then began backpedaling rapidly towards the door to the back. More thick, metallic clangs sounded from Chris/David's shield as she moved. As they approached a gap between the counters where they could be seen from the window, Amanda put on a burst of speed, hauling backwards with all of her might, building up an impressive head of steam in just a few, pumping steps.

They were almost all the way through when Debra's left leg jerked and new holes appeared in her pants. She cried out, apparently still conscious. Amanda redoubled her efforts, and hauled her to the door. She heard two meaty smacks as two new holes appeared in Debra's chest. She propped open the door with her hip and shoved Debra through it, then spun to dart in herself. Chris/David appeared, however, and almost bowled her over, rushing in.

A brief flash of panic at being locked out quickly gave way to a grudging sense of relief as David reached back out behind him and grabbed Amanda's arm, yanking her in and slamming the door closed behind her.

"We've got to move, quickly! If they're shooting in from the front, they've almost certainly got a guy around back. We need to get through him before they can send the guys in the front in to brace us from either side. Go, go!"

He pushed Amanda towards the back. But, she didn't even know where the rear exit was! And Debra! Amanda slapped his hand away from her. "Take an arm!" she snapped at him, ducking her head to get her neck under one of Debra's arms and standing up, bringing the limp older woman with her.

"No, stop, she's already dead! They shot her through the heart!"

Amanda opened her mouth to tell Chris/David to shut his, but then she noticed the vacant look in Debra's eyes. She held up a hand to her mouth, but felt no breath. "No, no no no…" she muttered as she sat the older woman back down and checked her pulse. Nothing.

"Come *ON!*" Chris/David said, grabbing Amanda's arm and yanking hard. He pulled her away from Debra's body. "Let's go, lady!"

Amanda's mind started to… Flicker. Everything seemed to happen under a strobe light, leaving her flashes of images that seems disconnected, unrelated. In between she saw shapes and colors.

Chris/David, grabbing her shoulder and spinning in front of her in the hallway.

Green rectangles growing and changing shape against a backdrop of white.

Chris/David's back, erupting into the golden light of sunset through the rear entrance.

Red triangles flew past blue squares.

She next saw him standing over a man in a suit who lay on his back on the asphalt, another suited man stumbling back, blood exploding out of his face as David drew back a fist.

White and yellow circles orbiting a purple pill shape.

She saw the mouth of the alley they'd exited into, where it met the street.

The green diamonds and orange stars faded, and the moments began to lengthen out and connect to each other. They rushed towards a car, whose doors opened for them. Chris/David dived in first and got himself behind the wheel. Amanda bundled in right after him, ending up sideways across the seat. The man didn't wait for her to fix herself, but punched the throttle and took off like a dart.

"Who are you?" He demanded, "And where did you hear the name David?"

Amanda opened her mouth to try to answer him, but then her vision abruptly went glittery and gold all over. She blinked, confused, but her eyelids made no difference to the scene before her.

Gradually, the even distribution of glittery gold began to resolve into lines and squares. One line sat at the horizon, maintaining its position even as her head moved, even though Amanda could not see the horizon for all the buildings whipping past. Another outlined the open door she was facing. A third formed a simple arrow pointing up.

Chris/David shouted "Close the door!"

Words began to appear, not glittering like gold, but shining with a glow that was the same shade of yellow as the lines.

Unknown speaker, the words by the arrow said.

Danger: open door on a moving vehicle, said the words by the door. More words were visible in her periphery.

    SBP: **119.7**
    HR: **128.3**
    T: **36.9**
    Crt: **1.2**
    UT: **19687385392**

Amanda didn't know what they meant. She stared, dumbfounded, her brain sluggish to respond.

`Visual communication restored.`

The voice! It was the voice! This was the visual communications it had spoken of! Amanda didn't like it. It was distracting. She willed it to turn off.

`Unable to disable visual communication at this time.`

Shit. She thought about it being fainter, less obtrusive.

"Uh," Amanda responded out loud, "I don't know, thinner, red lines!"

Chris/David looked at her like she was crazy. "What?" he asked, but Amanda ignored him.

The glittery and glowing golden color faded, becoming red and the lines of both the text and the shapes grew thinner.

She could see much better now. She kicked against the edge of the open door to spin her around in the seat, getting her feet down into the foot well. She leaned out and grabbed the door handle to pull it closed.

That's when the bus hit her.

At least, it felt like a bus. The impact came from behind and smacked Amanda straight forward. She bounced off the edge of the door painfully, then tumbled out. The car was moving at an impressive click, so she rolled and bounced across the asphalt.

Pain shot through her every time her body struck the ground. Not just the dull smack of impact, but hot, tearing, searing pain as she brushed the asphalt over and over, each time taking a layer of skin off. Her designer jeans tore further, exposing her knees and thighs to the damage, which dutifully happened as she tumbled and flailed.

After what felt like an eternity, a word flashed up in the center of her vision, in the red glowing lines.

This one didn't tumble and move with the rest of the world, remaining centered on her vision.

Flytrap

The pain was reduced. The blur of motion around here cleared up, and she could see what she was tumbling past. After a scant second of this minor respite, Amanda slammed into a trash can that had been bolted to the concrete sidewalk. She struck the thing with enough force to tilt it sideways, bending two of the four legs almost in half and bowing the others. More pain roared through her, originating in her back where she'd hit the box. She cried out and tried to curl up, but she couldn't move, so she lay still and let the darkness claim her.

Afraid

Monday, December 28th, 2759

Amanda awoke drowning. She jerked and flailed around, but something had her wrists, ankles, neck and waist held tight. She tried to cry out, but as soon as she drew in air to do so, water sprayed into her lungs and she coughed and wretched.

"Welcome back, darlin'," said a deep and cruel, nasally voice.

As her coughing fit subsided, she recognized that a wet washcloth was spread over her face. She could feel that she was laying on her back, on some sort of uncomfortable metal frame. That much, she could feel. She thought she saw a light through the washcloth. The whole experience carried with it a dreadful familiarity. She'd been here before; naked, tied down and afraid.

"What?" she called. "Where am I?"

"You should worry less about where you are, and more about why you're here." She felt a hand rest on her bare stomach and squirmed away from it. It was a large, rough hand that covered her from breasts to belly button.

"Why am I here?" she sputtered.

The voice laughed. It was a cold laugh, devoid of humor. She whimpered in response.

"You're here," the voice said, after a moment, "to answer my questions. And if you don't want 'here' to be the last place you ever see, you'll answer them honestly, understand?"

"Yes, I understand, I'll answer whatever questions you want..." Amanda's mind went into overdrive, trying to figure out what to do. Answering the man's questions was a no-brainer, but she worried she might not have enough answers to appease him.

She also suspected that he intended to kill her, regardless. The only thing that suggested otherwise was the washcloth, which obscured her vision. As she waited for him to begin asking questions, something abruptly obscured the light. She flinched, and then water poured onto her face.

She coughed and sputtered and panicked. She tried to breathe, but every breath brought a drowning sensation with it as she sucked droplets of water into her lungs. Somehow, she got enough air to scream, so she did.

After a moment, the water stopped. The soaked cloth still tried to drown her with every breath, so she continued to gag and cough for several minutes. When she was done, the rag was snatched away suddenly and bright light blinded her. She cried out again.

She kept her eyes squeezed shut for a moment until a large hand grabbed her chin. "Open your eyes, girl." Her eyelids fluttered open to reveal a face. He had deeply set, intelligent eyes that shone with cruelty and malice. His head was shaved bald, and he wore a goatee that completely covered the skin below his mouth.

She was in an unfinished brick room. Exposed pipes carried electricity and water around, and a bare bulb was the only light source. There were no windows, and a single door that she could see. She was strapped down to some frame she couldn't see with plastic zip ties.

He stepped back when she saw him and smiled coldly. "There we go. Now, we can have a conversation like reasonable people, right?"

Amanda stared, mute with fear.

"This isn't gonna work if you don't talk, darlin'," the man said.

"I-I-I understand," Amanda said. "We can t-talk, yes."

The man's smile broadened. "Good! So let's get started. The guy you were with. What's his name?"

Amanda's mind raced. She wanted to say "David", but the name he'd given her was different…

Cristobol Alvarez

The words appeared in her vision, and she became suddenly aware of the block of text in her periphery, as well.

"Chris!" she said, "Chris Alvarez, I think."

The man put his hands on his hips and shook his head. "Tsk, tsk tsk. That's not his name at all." He reached underneath her, and she felt him pinch one of the studs in the small of her back between his fingers.

"Wait!" she said, but he ignored her. He yanked down, the stud breaking free with a sharp pain that made her cry out. Tears filled her eyes and she sobbed while the man placed the bloody piercing on her belly. Amanda had flashes of painful memories. A man's rough hands on her body as she sobbed in pain. A woman's face, leering at her.

"You got some of these in some pretty sensitive places," the man said, grinning. She could smell his breath, and it stank of coffee and e-cigarettes. He ran a hand down her belly and stretched out two fingers between her legs to touch the piercing down there. "So I suggest you start telling the truth before I get to, say, this one."

He curled his finger and flicked the curved barbell between her legs, hard. The flick sent an electric jolt of pain through her and she tried to curl up again, to no avail.

"That's the only name I know! I swear to god!" she cried.

"Uh huh, We'll see. Where did you meet him?"

"I met him that night, right before you killed Debra!"

He reached under her again and yanked out the other stud. Amanda screamed.

As he placed the stud on her stomach next to the other one, he leaned down to speak quietly in her ear. "I want you to know that when you run out of piercings, things are going to get much, much worse. This is just a convenience for me, darlin'. I can do things that will make pulling one of these things out seem like an ant bite, in comparison. So do us both a favor and Stop. Fucking. Lying. Understand?"

"I'm not lying!" Amanda wailed, struggling to catch her breath. "I swear to god, I'm telling you the truth! I came to Debra's because I had some earrings that my boyfriend bought for me, and I needed money! To… To find him. He's missing. I was going to return them, and Debra said she knew him and would help me, she just needed to close the shop, but then that guy walked in and was talking to Debra and you killed her, and I ran with the guy out the back and then I fell out of his car and I woke up here! I promise, that's everything! That's all I know!"

The man paced around her for a moment before speaking. "That's funny. Real funny. Because you're feeding me the same damn story, but this time, I actually believe ya. So let's try something else. Tell me about your boyfriend. How did Chan know him?"

"I don't- I don't know. I think they grew up in the same neighborhood. She's older than he is, though."

"Uh huh. What's his name?"

"His name is Mike," Amanda said.

"Mike, huh? It's not Mike Flannigan, is it?"

The world seemed to bear down on her as the man said the name. It got colder, harder to breathe. The man watched her reaction and then pulled a phone out of his pocket and held it up to his ear. She heard him speak as he walked away from her.

"It's me. Listen, the target got away, but he had a girl with him. We managed to nab her. I've got her here, with me, and I'm asking questions. I was starting to think she didn't know anything, until she mentioned her boyfriend, and I got a name out of her. Mike fucking Flannigan."

He listened to the other person, "Well, sure, send me a picture," he said, then turned his phone to look at the screen. Amanda saw the light on his face change and he eyed it for a second before looking up at her. Her heart leapt into her throat. "Yep. That's her, all right."

He paced for a minute, listening. "Well, find out. I can pack her up to move, or get rid of her, or find out what she knows. I'll wait. And find out how much they're offering."

He stepped away and sat down on a small stool in the corner. He turned his face and eyes to the ceiling. Amanda could sense the impatience rolling off of him as he waited five, and then ten minutes. The whole time, her own apprehension grew. Someone was looking for her, and they didn't sound friendly.

Eventually, the man spoke again. "Yeah, I'm still here. I told you I'd wait. So what do they want?" Another pause followed. "Just the head? What are they gonna do, stick it on a pike by the door to the lobby? Fuck." The man laughed,a sick, disgusting sound that chilled Amanda to the bone. "Yeah, I can do it. See if you can get a hold of that guy at the waste processing plant, then. We'll need to get rid of the rest. We'll be there in an hour." Fear turned to panic. She realized, with sudden clarity, that she was going to die today, in this room, at the hands of this man. The injustice of it almost overwhelmed her until she felt something shift inside of her.

At the same time, her vision lit up with red letters.

Flytrap

He stepped back towards her, his movements slowed and oddly graceful in her elevated state. She waited until he was within arm's reach, one hand stretching out towards her face, the other moving behind his back. The plastic cuffs binding her to the frame stretched and snapped as she brought her arms up and grabbed the man by the neck, bringing his head down and hers up, crunching his nose into the top of her head. Bones and cartilage crunched and she felt hot blood in her hair almost immediately. The man let out a startled "oof!" and slammed a fist down into her stomach.

It knocked the wind out of her, but she didn't care about that at the moment. She kicked both legs, snapping the cuffs on her ankles and whipped her legs up and around his arm, and then his head. She clamped down, locking the man up in a position where he couldn't hit her anymore. Holding him there, she thrashed her torso and snapped the linked chain of plasticuffs around her waist, then concentrated hard on relaxing her diaphragm so she could suck in a deep breath.

The man struggled and pulled, but as big as he was, he didn't have the strength to break free. After a few seconds, she sucked in air, filling her lungs. She tensed the muscles in her neck and forced her head up, straining, stretching and finally breaking the last restraint. The release as the narrow plastic band cutting into her throat snapped was palpable, and she weakened her grip on the man just a bit.

It was enough. He whipped his head free of her and grabbed her by the hips, picking her up bodily and slamming her back into the frame. The metal struts shattered and collapsed beneath her. She grabbed one and slashed it into his arm with the speed of a striking snake.

The bones snapped with an audible crack and the man shouted in pain. She wedged a foot into his groin and shoved him away from her, then rolled backwards to her feet.

As soon as Amanda had her feet underneath her, she rushed forward, scooping up another metal bar with her other hand and whipping both into the man's ribs. The sound was like fireworks; a crackling of multiple bones all trying to break at once, but merely getting close. He roared even louder, so she cracked him across the face with a bar.

His yell was cut off by the blow, and he collapsed to the floor, insensate.

She heaved deep breaths as another word flashed in the center of her vision.

Daisy

The pain from her back returned in force, burning and itching lower down, burning and aching even more higher up. It was joined by a scratchy soreness in her wrists, waist and throat. Amanda dropped to her knees and sucked in air, trying to comprehend what just happened.

She wished for someone to talk to, even if just to explain all this strangeness to. Even the voice would be nice. She wondered what the words that flashed in front of her face meant.

The words are State Codes for Behavioral module 17c84f222a19000. Codes are being submitted to Behavioral module 17c84f222a19000 based on threat assessment values per the instructions included in Behavioral module 17c84f222a19000.

"What? You're doing this?"

The instructions included with Behavioral module 17c84f222a19000 include directives to CompanionAssist to submit State Code 'Flytrap' when threat assessment is at or above 72%, and, when State Code Flytrap is active, to submit State Code 'Daisy' when threat assessment is at or below 31%.

Amanda thought about it. The idea of the computer in her brain taking over and turning her into some kung-fu master was frightening, and she had no idea what other 'State Codes' existed.

"Can I submit the state codes myself?"

Yes. You may submit State Codes by directing the State Code at your CompanionAssist.

"So I just say the phrase?"

Vocalization is not necessary.

Amanda gasped. "What if I accidentally think them?"

Your CompanionAssist can distinguish between idle thoughts and commands.

Huh. She decided to try and sort this out now. She didn't know if anyone would come to investigate the ruckus she'd just caused, but no-one had yet, so she felt relatively safe for the moment.

She willed the voice to show her a list of all the State Codes, and it complied, writing them in her field of view.

Daisy - default behavior
Flytrap   - hand to hand combat, escape, evasion
Orchid - tradecraft
Rose   - psyops, honey trapping
Chamomile - infection

Amanda stared at the words for a while, then willed them away, and they obligingly vanished. The man on the floor was stirring and mumbling to himself. She had to move, now.

She tried the door, but it was locked. "Shit," she cursed, looking around. Her eyes rested on the man, who was quickly regaining consciousness. She rushed over and checked his pockets quickly, finding a set of keys in the front right pocket of his pants. She rushed back to the door and started trying keys.

She was three keys in when he shouted. "You bitch! You broke my fuckin' arm!"

She shrieked involuntarily and tried to move faster, but a massive weight slammed into her back and she tumbled to the floor.

"Flytrap!" she shouted, and the fear and pain vanished. She launched a kick into the man's leg, knocking him down beside her. He landed on his broken arm with a yell of pain and tried to grab her with the other. She quickly seized his good arm in an arm bar and arched her back with a smooth, quick jerk. His elbow shattered, eliciting a high-pitched scream that didn't match his appearance at all.

But Amanda didn't care. She leaned forward and wrapped his neck up in her arms, clamping down tightly, and then pushing her feet beneath her. The man was too frantic and hurt to offer much resistance, but he tried, flailing with both arms. She got herself upright, her left arm wrapped around the man's neck and clamping down, her right arm pushing up on her left hand.

She braced her feet, twisted her hips to the right, then jerked them to the left as hard as she could, throwing her legs out from underneath her at the same time. She came down hard, pain shooting up her left elbow, but the man's neck snapped and he stopped moving.

She stood and looked at the body and felt nothing. It occurred to her, distantly, that she had felt uncomfortable with this, but in the moment, it seemed unimportant. She retrieved the keys and quickly spotted one with the same manufacturer's mark as the bolt on the door. She inserted it and it turned easily.

She stepped out into a hallway in an unfinished office building. She pulled her location from her BCI and noted that she was in Tuen Mun district, about twelve kilometers from the jewelry shop. She walked forward with purpose, searching for where they had stashed her clothes. A sense of uneasiness started to form within her, but she ignored it.

She checked two more rooms before she found it, being guarded by a young street thug. He spun when he heard the door open behind him and pulled a gun from his waistband, but she snatched it and shot him through the heart. The gun was a cheap, electric semi-automatic with a twenty-round magazine. It was a knockoff, a lookalike of the centuries-old original Colt 1911, made by some unknown mom-and-pop manufacturer, likely right here in the city of New Kowloon.

But it was a gun, and it had eighteen rounds left in the magazine and one in the rails. She shook out her clothes and checked her purse. Everything was there, even her earrings and cash. She turned to the dead guard and patted him down quickly. She found $43 and another cheap pocket knife.

With a flash of inspiration, she grabbed the body's leg and held her foot up to the sole of one of his combat boots. Close enough. She left her designer boots behind and took his, which looked much more ruggedly built. The whole time, the uneasy feeling grew.

When she was finally fully dressed, she headed outside. Another guard stood there, facing out, not noticing her. She raised her stolen gun and shot him, the large, subsonic round making more noise as it penetrated his skull than it did being launched. She flipped the safety on and stuffed the gun into her belt at the small of her back as she approached the body. She patted him down.

He had a gun as well, but it was a different caliber. She briefly considered taking both weapons, but decided that the hassle of carrying them without holsters was too much. One was enough. She looked around for possible witnesses, but half of the street was in a state of decay, and the other half was unfinished construction. This must be one of the make-work projects the city engaged in periodically, hiring construction companies to tear down and rebuild a block, paying extra to ensure they hired local unskilled labor for the project.

She picked a direction that would take her back towards the Jewelry shop, where she hoped to find the address of Debra's cousin and their in-law suite. As she walked, the uneasy feeling grew even stronger, until it finally cracked her artificially-induced calm.

Daisy, she sent to her BCI.

Amanda collapsed to her knees and cried out in pain as all the hurts returned. A puddle lay in the gutter next to her, and she could see her face was bruised and scraped from the tumble out of the car. She choked back a sob at her own appearance, and cursed the stupid computer in her head.

It may have saved her life, but she was becoming more and more convinced that it had played a large role in what had happened to her, anyways. She just wanted to find Mike and forget all of this. Maybe her amnesia was anterograde… She remembered a film about a man with anterograde amnesia. It precluded one from forming new memories. It sounded almost blissful at this point, but she recalled that it had only taken about five or ten minutes for the memories to fade in the film. She sighed and pushed herself to her feet.

Going to the jewelry store seemed like a bad idea, now. But when she was unemotional a moment ago, it had seemed like a good idea, so she was torn. She tried to think of what to do, instead, but came up with nothing. She didn't know anyone except Chris/David, Mike and Debra, and Debra was dead. She didn't know how to find either Mike or Chris/David.

With a flash, she realized that she'd just remembered something from before. The movie! She thought back on it now, and tried to move out from there.

She had seen it while sitting on a couch with Mike. She was sure of that. She tried to picture the room, but they'd had the lights off. She felt like she knew the room, but try as she might, she couldn't get any more than that. After a few moments of trying to recall, she gave up.

She sat down on the curb and stuck her hands in her pockets. Her right hand brushed something, and she pulled it out. It was her receipt from the makeup purchase. And there, written across the top was a phone number.

She didn't know what else to do. She didn't have anyone else to call. She was beginning to feel like a broken record, bouncing from one person to the next, begging for help, but she didn't know what else she could do. With a deep sigh, she imagined calling the number and directed the thought at the voice.

Accepted

Monday, December 28th, 2759

An hour and a half later, an expensive-looking, compact sports car pulled up and the passenger door opened to reveal Sasha behind the wheel. As soon as her eyes landed on Amanda, they flashed wide.

"Oh my god! Get in! What happened?"

Amanda stood, every bone in her body protesting, every muscle aching, her skin burning under her clothes. She took the two slow steps to the car door, and then collapsed in.

"Thank you," she said, drawing the door closed.

"What happened?" Sasha asked again, pulling away with a spin of the tires and accelerating quickly up to a thoroughly unsafe speed. "Wait, first, do you need a hospital?"

"No," Amanda responded. "I don't have enough money for a hospital. I need a place to hide. You can take me to…"

She stopped. She didn't know where she could go. "A hotel," she said, after a moment's thought.

"What? Don't you at least want to go home?"

"I don't… I don't know where my home is. It wouldn't be safe, anyways."

Sasha stared at her for a moment. She seemed to be calculating something, or maybe just processing what Amanda had just said. "Well, then you're coming home with me," she said with sudden conviction. Amanda looked over in surprise. "I have enough money for a hotel, it's okay-"

"No! You're hurt! Who did that to you?"

Amanda opened her mouth to answer, but a sudden vertigo swept through her. Her head began to spin and she slumped down even further into the seat as everything went black.

Amanda woke with the vehicle still in motion, so she couldn't have been out for too long. Even at night, the sidewalks that flashed past were crowded with people. "What happened?" she muttered, her words slurred.

"You just passed the fuck out!" Sasha exclaimed, "I'm glad you're back, though, because you really had me worried. Like, I was *really* scared.

"Amanda, right? Well, Amanda, you don't look so good. I thought for sure you just fucking *died* on me and I was driving around with a corpse in my car. And I don't even know your last name, and the cops would arrest me if I went to them, so I was freaking out for a second there!" She ended with a rather manic laugh.

"I'm okay, " Amanda said, "I'm just... I'm injured, but I just need to rest." She stared out the window, looking at the crowds like birds on the bank of a fast-flowing river.

Sasha balked, "You need a fucking doctor."

"I can't afford a doctor..."

"Well, I'm gonna be one in two years. So..."

Amanda laughed, which hurt like hell. "You're a medical student?"

"Yeah. One more year of school and a year of residency, and I'll be a doctor."

"Do you have medical supplies at home?" Sasha nodded enthusiastically and smiled. "I only work at Cindy's because my grant agreement requires me to have a job. 'Real work experience' or something like that. It's stupid. I mean, I'll be working in a hospital when I finish school, and a hospital is nothing like retail. But 'them's the rules', as they say, so I do it. It's a little extra money, which is nice, because I have a habit to feed."

Amanda eyed her up and down. She tried to think of what sort of drugs an excitable medical student would take.

"Neuroplasticizers?" she asked after a moment's thought. She didn't know where the word had come from, and was too beat down to care.

"What? No, I don't..." Sasha barked another nervous laugh, "Sorry, I have a *shopping* habit. I impulse buy. Like a lot, haha. I mean, a *lot*. It's one of the reasons my mom let me go to medical school instead of law school, like my step-dad. Because doctors make good money too, haha. She said I'll need plenty of money to take care of myself, since I've got *zero* interest in hooking up with some rich guy who'll take care of me, the way mom did."

"Do you have any... Any painkillers? Like with you?"

Sasha looked over and her face twisted in a sympathetic expression. "Nothing potent, I'm sorry. I don't like to drive around with stuff like that, because it's how you get robbed. I have some mild analgesics in my purse, for like, period cramps and headaches. You can have those. They're the nice stuff, so there's no downside to taking too many." She stuck a hand down between the seats and retrieved a rhinestone-encrusted, black leather clutch bag, which she held out to Amanda.

As Amanda took the bag, Sasha made a right turn onto a narrow street. The momentum from such a sharp turn at their high speeds pushed Amanda into Sasha, the seatbelt digging in painfully. She let out a pained gasp and whimpered quietly. "Do you think you can slow down a little?"

"What? Oh! Okay, yeah, haha. Sorry, when I saw what you looked like I was like 'Okay, Sasha, we need to beat feet the hell out of there, right fucking now', So I just, like, punched it. But I can slow down, sure, no problem."

She did so, bringing the zippy vehicle down to a relatively sedate thirty kilometers over the limit. Amanda looked at the crowds again, and noticed that the well-dressed, happy people she had seen earlier that day were nowhere to be seen. Only the stressed looking folks were still out and about, moving around in sullen or angry walks, eyes down or glaring around, looking for trouble.

She tore her eyes away from the masses and dug through the purse. It contained an impressive assortment of makeup and at least three thousand dollars in cash, in addition to a pocket wallet stuffed with various credit and debit cards. Amanda supposed the happy people still out and about were all in the cars they whipped around and left in their wake.

There, at the bottom, she found a prescription bottle with the label half ripped off. The remaining label identified it as a twelve-year-old prescription for an emergency contraceptive, issued to "...sha Greenfield". She opened it and saw a handful of tiny, blue pills.

Small, round, blue pill with white lettering 'N5' and RFID resonance of 5.7294 GHz. Neoprophen, 5mg. Typical adult dosage is 10mg.

Amanda supposed it was nice that the voice was making itself useful. She remembered Sasha's invitation and shook out six of them, tilting her head back and throwing them in her mouth. It took a serious effort to swallow them dry, but she did it and ignored the lingering choking sensation.

Out of curiosity, she dug through the pocket wallet and found a physical ID card. Sasha Greenfield, who was a last-year medical student, worked at Cindy's Boutique, was quite attractive, a little socially awkward and had needed an emergency contraceptive twelve years ago. She frowned, the math not adding up.

"How old are you?" she asked. Sasha smiled. "I'm twenty-two. And you?"

"I, uh… I don't know, actually."

"You don't know! Oh my god, are you a war orphan?!" Sasha's eyes widened and Amanda curiously prodded at the voice, to see if it could explain.

Arthesian war orphans. According to Wikipedia, the Arthesian war orphans are the approximately 40 percent of children born in the People's Republic of Arthesia between the start of the Tripartite War, in January of 2721 and the signing of the Treaty of New Kowloon, in March of 2727.

"Uh, no, I don't think I'm quite that old."

"What? How do you not know how old you are, then?"

"I…" Amanda paused. She was reluctant to drag Sasha into this. Everything about her seemed so innocent and pure; her nervous laugh, the way she yammered on and on, the immediate and unconditional offer of aid… And the last person she'd opened up to was dead now. Debra had held herself like a domineering, proper matron, but she'd exposed a caring side to Amanda. And then Amanda got her killed.

"Well?" Sasha asked. She was looking at Amanda expectantly. Amanda winced, tried to come up with a lie, and then had a realization. It didn't matter. She'd already dragged Sasha into whatever she was involved in when she made the phone call. She finally allowed herself to do the math, and admitted what she'd already know. Sasha had gotten pregnant at 10. And ten-year-old girls generally didn't get pregnant from their own bad choices. Sasha knew what it meant to be hurt.

Besides, withholding information now would only make it more dangerous for her.

"I… Lost my memory. I don't remember anything before I woke up in an alley last night. I was naked and covered in blood. All I can remember are a couple of names and…" she laughed at the absurdity of it. "A movie I watched once. About a character with amnesia."

Sasha frowned. "You don't remember *anything* before last night?"

"Just what I said. My name, two more names, and sitting on a couch, watching a movie."

"But that's not how amnesia works, hun." Sasha's voice was much more level now. She sounded less nervous, more self-assured. Amanda guessed it was the medical talk that drew this out.

"Yeah. In retrograde amnesia, you usually don't lose your oldest memories. In fact, you usually don't lose more than a few minutes, or in some rare cases, memories about a specific subject. And memory recovery almost always takes one of two paths; either you start recovering memories soon after, like within a matter of hours, or you just never recover anything. The kind of spotty flashes that you're telling me about sound like something out of a movie."

Amanda stared blankly, trying to process what Sasha was saying. "So what you're saying is that, if I'm remembering anything, I should be remembering a lot more?"

Sasha shrugged "Or just not remembering anything at all. But most amnesia is temporary, even anterograde amnesia. Total retrograde amnesia, followed by remembering little bits here and there over the course of a full day following the onset is more fiction than reality. Unless…"

Amanda perked up. "Unless what?"

"No, I don't want to be rude."

"I won't be upset with you, I promise. Please, I don't know what's been happening to me, anything you can tell me might help."

"Well… There is a kind of amnesia that works more or less the way it does in the movies… It's caused by traumatic experiences. Like… Emotionally traumatic experiences."

Amanda slouched down in her seat and thought about that. She had figured she'd fallen off a building, or been hit in the head, or injected with something, or maybe -given the burn marks on her chest- subjected to an electric shock. But from what Sasha was saying, her memory should be returning by now, if that were the case.

The problem was that she *knew* she'd been subjected to some form of violence. The scrapes on her knees and elbows and knuckles, the burn marks, the blood… That was the proof. But a psychological trauma might explain her amnesia.

She thought about the small room with the ugly, leering man. Was this, perhaps, her second time in such a room?

"Do you, ah… Do you want to tell me what happened to you? Tonight? Or maybe, uh… You know. Before?" Sasha's voice was tentative now, and laced with concern.

"It's a long story, hun," Amanda said with a sigh.

"Well, it's a long drive. Hour and a half. You could tell me, or you could sit here listening to me yammer on and on about whatever pops into my head. I'm serious, by the way. I will talk your ears off. I can't stop, especially when I get nervous, and I thought you died just a minute ago, and even though you're still alive, you're hurt and dirty and you need help, and I don't know what's going on so I'm in, like, full yammer-yammer mode, here." She paused for breath and then fixed Amanda with a sober look.

"You see?"

Amanda laughed again. She couldn't help it. Sasha was almost like a child demanding attention. And it was endearing. There was something about the woman that spoke to Amanda. She wasn't sure if it was her inoffensive personality, her curvaceous good looks or just the simple, open and honest expressions that shaped her features. Whatever it was, Amanda actually felt like she could trust her, despite barely knowing a thing about her.

She didn't know anything. She didn't know how to assess a threat or danger. But she knew how she felt.

So Amanda laid it all out. From waking up in the alley to her escape from the torture room. She didn't leave anything out, admitting to the four people she'd killed in the past day, her desperation to find Mike and piece her life back, the death of Debra and the mysterious Chris/David figure, who'd shown up, saved her life, and then vanished. She told Sasha about the voice, the State Codes, everything.

When she was done, they drove in silence for a while.

"Does your BCI have any record of anything before you woke up?"

"No. Every time I've thought about it, it tells me that 'Logs prior to Dec 26 2759 - 21:40:56 UTC are corrupted and inaccessible'," she answered, mimicking the robotic tones of the voice.

"What's the boot log say?"

"The what?" Amanda asked.

"The boot log. So, it's kept separate from the activity logs because it's kind of important, since it's a computer in your brain and you need to know if it's working, or got reset or something."

"How do you know all this?"

Sasha glanced over, her face a mask of concern. "I'm a medical student. BCIs are medical implants. I had to take a class on them for my GP track."

Amanda focused her thoughts on the voice and wished for it to show her its boot logs. Red letters appeared in front of her and she read them off.

"There's just two dates. December 8th, 2758, 07:03:41 UTC. December 26th, 2759, 21:40:49 UTC."

"Wait, what was the timestamp you said the logs were corrupted before?"

Amanda asked the voice.

"21:40:56," she answered.

"Well, there's a seven second difference there."

"I don't know what that means."

"It means something happened in those seven seconds that is probably what corrupted the logs. And since you have a BCI, and there's no telling what kind of neural-interface it has, it might be responsible for your memory loss."

Amanda sat up straight, the seat belt tightening in alarm at her motion.

"Oh my god, Sasha! You're amazing, I never even thought of that!"

Sasha grinned, proud of herself. "Well, I am almost a doctor, so don't be too surprised."

Amanda grinned back.

"When we get there, I have a neuro-imager and a quantic wireless transceiver, so maybe I can do something about it? I don't know, but at least we can take a look inside your head and see if we can see what's going on. And I can do something about…" she gestured vaguely at Amanda with one hand and Amanda nodded. "The rest of me, yeah. Thank you, Sasha. I really just called you for a ride, I don't know what to say to all of this."

Sasha gave her shoulders a happy little shake, excited to have a purpose. "Thank you is fine. Don't take this the wrong way, but you really look like you could use a friend and a little help. It's no big deal, really."

Amanda just smiled at her. She didn't really know how big of a deal it was, but as for needing a friend… She certainly couldn't disagree with that.

An hour later, Sasha put down the neuro-imager and stared blankly at Amanda.

"You're not human," she said.

"What?" That didn't make sense, Amanda thought. Of course she was human.

"Your brain is about this big," Sasha held up two fingers, about six centimeters apart, "and the rest of your head is full of lipids and computer equipment."

"What?" Amanda asked again, not understanding.

"Look for yourself," Sasha turned the display on the imager around and touched a button. An indecipherable mess of black lines and washes of colors on an off-white background greeted her, squirming around like worms inside of an outline of her head. "I can't understand what I'm seeing."

Sasha put a finger on the display. "This is your BCI. It's a fairly standard model for the military or high-level software developers. And this," she shifted her finger over a few centimeters to point at a blue-ish tinted mass of wiggling lines, "is your actual brain. You'll notice that it's quite small, and consists of your medulla, pons, midbrain, temporal lobe, hypophysis, optic nerve and a few other structures, mostly related to lower-level autonomous functionality and sensory perception. And then there's these," she moved her finger again, to indicate a large grouping of wiggling lines overlaid onto reddish, straight lines, "...which are all computers. I'm not a computer expert, but I know a thing or two, and there's enough processing power in there to substitute for the rest of your brain, easily."

"Is that why I can't remember anything? Why my symptoms aren't normal for people with amnesia?"

Sasha shrugged. "I don't know. Like I said, I'm not a computer expert."

"Why would all that stuff be in my head in the first place?"

Sasha shrugged again. "Well, if I didn't already know better, I'd swear you were one of those skin job bots. But you're clearly not, soooo…

"TBI, maybe? You might have had a TBI while in a virtual environment or something. If it damaged your brain, your mind would be fine for as long as you were in the environment, but if you exited it into a damaged brain; boom. Instant vegetable. But if that happened and you got help before you exited the environment, they might have been able to just keep you in the environment while they implanted enough computing power to make a functioning brain for you to return to."

"What's a TBI?" Amanda asked.

"Oh, sorry, Traumatic Brain Injury."

Amanda nodded thoughtfully. "So you think I might have been injured while I was plugged into a… A virtual environment, you said? I don't even know what that is…"

"You don't know what a virtual environment is?"

"No, should I?"

Sasha put the imager down and sat down on her couch next to Amanda. "They're virtual reality environments; whole worlds programmed into a massive computer with enough power to simulate thousands, or even millions or billions of human brains. The Transhumanist Collective builds big ones, called Digital Arcologies, and sets them into orbit around young stars. The idea is to let people 'immigrate' by jacking in and then killing their bodies off. Once in, you're basically immortal, and if you want out, you just pick a robot body. Maybe that's where you're from. I've never heard of them using skin-jobs, but it's possible."

"I feel like I would know if I was involved with one of those. I feel like I'm from here, not just this planet, but this city, New Kowloon."

"Why do you think that?"

"I recognized someone's accent. And it's not just that. I just, kinda, *feel* like I'm from here. The whole city feels familiar to me."

"Huh."

"What was the other thing you said? A skin job bot?" Amanda asked.

"Oh, I'm sure you're not one of those sex bots. I've met some, and you look like one of the models, but you don't act *at all* like them. Guys like to bring them into Cindy's and pick out their makeup for them. They all act like lovesick hookers, rubbing all over the guy and stuff. It's the way they're programmed; they're designed to get just super attached and clingy to one guy, and to have this drive to please him that never goes away. There's nothing else to their personality but that codependent attachment. They say there's more to them than that, that they're just like real women, but I've never seen it. It's honestly creepy as shit, because they look totally real, but for guys who have the money…"

"Yeah, that sounds creepy. I'm sure I'm not a sex bot, I'm just…" She sighed. Now she not only didn't know *who* she was, she didn't know *what* she was, either.

"Well," Sasha said, "You'll need a computer expert to take a look at what's in your head, in any event. Meanwhile, I can take a look at the rest of you. Go ahead and strip, I'm going to get my stuff and I'll be right back."

Amanda stood stiffly as Sasha walked through an archway into the kitchen. It was a nice apartment, she thought. It wasn't too small, and Sasha had good tastes. All the furniture was antiqued faux wood stuff with wrought iron trim, lots of black iron set against dark brown wood. It gave the place a warm, welcoming vibe that was only enhanced by the mess. Papers and books and tablets and clothes were strewn about, covering one side of the couch, two of the three chairs at the small dining table, half of the dining table itself, and parts of the kitchen counter. The place was lived in.

She stripped off her clothes slowly, wincing as she peeled away layers that were stuck to her skin with dried blood. She spotted a plastic bag laying on the coffee table, so she folded them and placed them on it. She put her stolen gun on top.

Sasha had wanted to do this part first, but Amanda had insisted on checking out her head, and the other woman had relented after a brief argument.

When Sasha returned, she stopped and gasped. "Oh, wow. That's worse than I thought. You should have listened to m- Is that a gun?!" Amanda nodded sheepishly. "I took it from... From one of the men who hurt me."

Sasha shook her head to clear it and busied herself opening her medical kit and pulling stuff out.

Bandages, tubes of cream and something that looked like a small drill with a tiny mirror where there drill bit would normally go.

"What's that? The drill-thing," Amanda asked.

"Tissue regenerator. It's not the best one out there, but it's what I could afford to keep here. It's gonna itch, like a lot, but you really need… Actually, you really need a shower, first. If there's any foreign material in your wounds, we need to get it out first, or you'll get an infection. Come on." Sasha beckoned her to the kitchen. Amanda followed her through the kitchen and then through another door into a bathroom with a shower stall.

"Don't use my regular body washes, they have organics in them," Sasha said as she opened the cabinet under the sink and began digging underneath it. "Here," she said, holding out a bottle with a plain white label full of ten syllable words in blocky print. "This is antibiotic soap. It won't sting your cuts, either. Do… Do you need help?"

Amanda turned on the shower and waited for it to warm up. "I…" She paused, thinking. A part of her wanted Sasha to join her. She recalled the other woman's mannerism during their first encounter; flirtatious. And the kind, caring person she'd caught a glimpse of tonight made that flirting rather appealing.

"Yes. Please," she said, very softly, watching Sasha through her eyebrows. Sasha undressed without a word, and they stepped into the tiny shower together.

Amanda cleaned her sides and front and let Sasha scrub the blood and sweat off of her back. A moment after Sasha gasped.

"What is it?" Amanda asked, trying to look over her shoulder and failing to spot anything but the top of Sasha's head.

"It's, uh… It's a GSW. A bullet wound. You've been shot!"

"That must have been what knocked me out of the car," Amanda muttered.

"Knocked you out of the… Wait, stop. Okay, just… Just let me clean you up, and then I'll see what I can do, medically. Jesus… You're lucky you survived all of this. Did… Did you get stabbed in the small of your back? With an icepick or something?"

"No," Amanda said, wincing at the memory, "Those were piercings. The guy interrogating me ripped them out."

"Jesus, girl… I'm dying to know what's going on too, but I can't imagine doing stuff like this to find out… You're lucky to be alive, you know that? Or else you're the toughest bitch I ever met."

Amanda snorted a rueful laugh that sent stabbing pain through her chest and sides. "I'm just me."

"Well, that much is clear," Sasha replied, her tone distracted as she rubbed at a particularly thick crust of blood, "It's just that the 'just me' part is a shockingly tough bitch. Okay, I'm done. Have you scrubbed off your front?" Amanda turned around and found herself face to face with Sasha. She had intended to answer in the affirmative, but the feel of her, wet and naked, and pressed against Amanda's own body drove all thought from her mind.

Amanda leaned down just a little bit and kissed her, tentatively. Sasha didn't react, but watched Amanda, her lips parted slightly and trembling. Amanda thought she looked scared but when Amanda drew back, she lifted a finger and touched her lip, experimentally. As if she was checking to make sure it was really her that Amanda had kissed.

She shifted her finger to Amanda's lips and traced them, slowly, starting at the bottom of her lips and circling around. When she finished, she drew her finger down Amanda's chin, down her throat, across her clavicle and between her breasts and curved away to the side as her other hand came up. She rested both hands on Amanda's hips and leaned forward, her breasts pressing gently into Amanda's ribs.

Amanda kissed her again, with more confidence this time. She felt the delicate texture of Sasha's lips, pressed against her own, and tasted them with the tip of her tongue. Sasha's hands moved, and she squeezed gently. Right on a couple of bruises.

Amanda hissed in pain, and flinched back.

"Oh my god!" Sasha exclaimed, the spell broken, her eyes widening, "I'm so sorry! I didn't mean to- You know what? We need to get you patched up and taken care of. This is unprofessional of me. I should be taking care of you, not... Ugh. You started it. Come on, listen to your doctor. "

"It's okay," Amanda tried to assure her, but Sasha wasn't listening. "Come on," she said, reaching around Amanda to turn off the water. "Let's go to my bedroom. You can lay on my bed while I work on your back. That's where the worst of it is."

Amanda closed her mouth and let Sasha lead the way.

Sasha's bedroom was a cluttered mess, but there was a pattern to it that suggested that the young woman knew where everything was. Amanda waited while Sasha moved a few articles of clothing off the bed and then pulled back the sheets, throwing down a towel. Amanda laid down on it and Sasha pulled her desk chair out, shoving papers off the desk and replacing them with her medical kit.

"Okay, I'm going to finish cleaning the wounds. You're still bleeding, which isn't great, but it's not a lot of blood. Your blood pressure was okay when I checked you before, so fingers crossed. If this bullet is holding a nicked artery shut, this could get bad. I can probably fix it, but I don't have any blood to give you. At best, you'll be off your feet for a week."

Amanda felt Sasha probing at the middle of her back and down where the piercings had been. It hurt, but she kept quiet and let the woman work. Sasha continued to talk as she worked.

"The GSW is just off the centerline, and there's no exit wound. Barely missed your spine. I'm frankly shocked that it didn't kill you. That's right where your heart is. It must have missed all the major arteries, which is like a one in a million shot. I'm going to have to remove the bullet, but I've got plenty of lidocaine and even some pseudo-opiates, so it shouldn't be too bad. So you might feel a couple of little pinches in just a second here, try not to squirm too much. How's that?" Amanda felt a little pinch between her shoulder blades.

"It's fine," she responded, "Okay," Sasha said, "Good, because I'm going to have to do it a bunch more before I can get the bullet out." Amanda felt the pinch repeat itself a half dozen times. "Okay, that's nine injections, the site should be pretty numb, but that's just the skin and the top layer of muscle. I'm going to give you some pseudo-opiates now. Let me know when they kick in, okay?" Amanda felt another, sharper pinch, this one in her butt cheek. "Ow!" she exclaimed, not expecting it.

"Sorry! The opiate needle has to be bigger than the lidocaine one. And it needs to go into a big mass of muscles, so..." Sasha rubbed gently at the spot as a wave of warm tingling rushed through Amanda. There was something oddly familiar about the feeling of Sasha's hand on her ass, but the spread of warmth from the drugs made it hard to concentrate.

"I think it's kicking in," she said.

"Okay, here we go. Sasha quieted down after that and Amanda tried her best to relax. Sasha proceeded to roughly yank her lungs out of the wound. Or at least that's what it felt like. The thing Sasha produced wasn't a lung, however, but a small, misshapen hunk of tungsten and steel that was unceremoniously dropped on the desk next to the bed.

She continued, cleaning the small wounds at Amanda's lower back and then producing a tissue regenerator and running it over her back. More tugging followed as Sasha put stitches in the wound.

"Okay, that's the best I can do for the GSW. There's some damage to your ribs, but the bullet managed to slip between two of them. I'll hit it with the tissue regenerator again in the morning to help get it started healing. Now, roll over and let me check your front."

Amanda complied and Sasho looked her over. "No tattoos, but you, uh, really like your piercings, huh?" She brought the tissue regenerator over the various bruises and minor cuts and scrapes. A bright beam of light and a slight hum emanated from the device when Sasha squeezed the trigger.

"I guess. I don't really remember getting any of them."

"I've thought about getting my nipples pierced, but every time I've had the opportunity to get it done, I chicken out…"

"Why?" Amanda asked, propping herself up on her elbows.

"Well," Sasha turned her face down, but her eyes lingered on Amanda. "It just feels.. Silly. With no-one to…" She wiggled a finger in a vague gesture. Amanda looked down and flicked one of the balls at the end of one nipple piercing. "You can do that to me, if you like."

Sasha grinned at her and touched the barbell with the tip of one finger. She slid her hand around

Amanda's breast and onto her side, giving her a squeeze. "Hurt?"

"No, the drugs are working well." In fact, the touch felt wonderful.

"Opiates feel pretty good, huh?"

"Not as good as you." Amanda leaned forward and kissed her. Sasha kissed back and they sunk back down onto the bed.

Addled

Tuesday, December 29th, 2759

Amanda woke to Sasha staring at her.

"You're not human."

Amanda blinked and rubbed her eyes. "You said that already. You told me it could have been a TBI while I was-"

"No, that time I was being metaphorical. Even if that happened, you'd still be human. This time, I'm being literal. Look." Sasha turned the screen of the device she was staring at to Amanda. It showed a graph of some sort; a series of vertical lines of varying height. "Uh, what?"

"It's your DNA. It's not human."

"How can you tell?" Amanda sat up and peered at the screen.

"Look," Sasha said again, and tapped the screen a few times. The graph split in half and one side rearranged itself. The bottom showed labels; 'Subject' on the left and 'Human (mainline)' on the right.

"Um, they don't look that different to me..." Sasha pointed to a number below the labels, one of several. It was labeled 'Match' and it read 43.8.

"So I'm forty-three point eight percent human? Is that weird?"

"Not if you're a banana… Listen, *chimpanzees* share 98.8 percent of their DNA with humans. Genetically speaking, you're *way* more different from a human than that. You're.. Something else."

"Are you sure that thing's accurate?" Amanda frowned, "It sounds like there was some… Contamination or something." She thought about the Behavioral State code, Chamomile. Contagion.

"No, I calibrate it every time I use it. This is the second time I've ran some of your blood, and I ran some of mine in between to check it."

"So what am I, then? Can that thing tell?"

Sasha nodded. "Yeah, gimme a second."

She fiddled with it for a moment, then stopped and her eyes went wide. "Oh, wow! That's cool! But…" She continued to tap at the screen while Amanda grew impatient.

"What? What does it say?"

"Oh! Uh, so I guess you're, like, *mostly* a Draughtgen, but not entirely. And I think the rest is human, but I'm not sure. I'd need to run an expression sim, and I don't have the equipment to do that…"

"What?" Amanda fell back to the bed, confused and still sleepy.

"Okay, so it says you're ninety-nine point three percent Draughtgen. The rest doesn't line up precisely in a one-to-one manner with the equivalent parts of the human genome, but each little chunk *can* be lined up with parts of the human one, except for these thirty-two sections… They look weird. I'm not a geneticist, but they look artificial. But like I said, you're mostly Draughtgen. Am I saying that right? It can be hard to pronounce a lot of their- I mean your words with all the consonants stacked up the way they do it.”

Amanda fixed her eyes on the ceiling, noting the texture of the finish and the slightly off white color. “I have no idea. I don't even know what that is.”

“Oh, yeah. Amnesia…” Sasha sat quietly for a moment, then spoke in a gentle voice.

“Amanda, I think we need to revisit that whole skin-job bot idea. Your genome… It's not natural.”

“You don't think I'm just a draw- a Draughtgen with a human great-grandfather or something?”

“Humans and Draughtgen can't breed, hun. You can get in-vivo gene therapy to change from one to the other, but there's no real in-between. No, your body was built, not born. I don't know how you got yourself in it, but… I mean, Amanda, you're not even a sexbot…”

“Hold on, I'm really confused here,” Amanda could feel her heart beginning to race as her brain struggled to process the mix of radical ideas and new words.

“Start from the beginning. What's a Draughtgen?”

“The Draughtgen are the first artificial subspecies of humans. They're old, like really old. Like pre Diaspora old. They were literally designed to be super soldiers, so they're stronger and faster than normal humans and better at, like, tactical stuff, I guess. They heal fast, and they take longer to develop and they live longer than normal people. I met one, once, who was like, twenty-five years old and she looked like she was fifteen.”

"Okay, so they look like normal people?"

Sasha smiled a little ruefully, "Well, yeah. I mean, look in a mirror. I'm guessing you're like, forty years old? Because you look like you're about twenty. But you could be fifty, for all I know. Or you could be a couple days old, if they grew your body in a vat." Sasha reached out and stroked Amanda's chest and sides. "God, I've always loved your body." Sasha cut the last word off abruptly.

The touch gave Amanda a little thrill, but the words were odd. Always? What did that mean? Amanda asked, "Always?" eyeing Sasha with interest.

Sasha's cheeks flushed and she looked away. "I may have been watching you bend over in the store yesterday. There's a chance I may have been picturing what was under your jeans. It's a possibility. No way to know, really."

"Enough flattery." Amanda said, swatting Sasha's arm gently. "'ll let you play with my body after we talk. So why did you say you don't think my body is a sex-bot body. I'm a young woman, which is exactly what most sex-bots would be, right?"

"Yeah, well, I mean, there's a lot of young male sex-bots, too, but female bots are more common. And I've heard of a few modeled after middle-aged men or women, but that's a pretty niche market, I bet. It's your genes, girl. Even if you were a sex-bot from the Empire, where I'm pretty sure skin-job bots are illegal, you'd be 100% Draughtgen, because why would they bother doing anything else?"

Amanda frowned. "The Empire? What empire?"

"The United Empire of Earth. It was founded by the Draughtgen. It's not really an empire, more of a federal democracy, but they have a ceremonial Emperor, so… Empire. It's a really big nation, like the second or third largest in the galaxy. Hundreds of billions of citizens, about half of them Draughtgen.

"But like I said, even if you were from there, which would be illegal because they're huge on giving sapient AIs full rights and stuff, why would they modify your genes? I mean, the sex-bots, they use normal human genetics. Instead, your genome looks like what some genetic engineer might come up with for a… A, uh… A combat skin-bot."

"A combat skin-job? Does that even make sense? Wouldn't a metal combat bot be better?"

"Yes? I think? I don't know, I'm not a… A military… Design… Person, you know what I mean. I would think that a metal bot would be a lot better, because it would be stronger. But if you *had* to be organic, for some reason… They might tweak your DNA so that you could pass as human, or to try and improve on some trait the Draughtgen have. That would explain why you're not 100% Draughtgen."

"Okay, so maybe your TBI theory from last night still works? Like I was injured *really* badly, but my mind was being simulated by a computer, so I got a whole new body?"

"Yes. That sounds about right. I mean it makes sense. I can't tell if that's what happened based on this, though."

Something occurred to Amanda. "Sasha, yesterday morning, after I left your store, I went to a jewelry shop, and the owner mistook me for a sex-bot, I think. He called me..." She thought for a moment, trying to recall his words. Her BCI provided them by way of a recording that played back in her head.

"A Viridian Seven series Companion."

"Well, let's look them up." Sasha reached over Amanda and retrieved her phone from the table. She held it up and said "Show me pictures of Viridian Seven series Companions." The screen came on and both women gasped at what appeared on it.

They were pictures of Amanda. She had different hairstyles and her makeup was done differently in every image, but each face in the gallery on the screen was the same face that she'd seen in every reflective surface since she woke up in the alley.

"So my mind got stuck in a sex-bot's body?"

Sasha looked back and forth between the screen and Amanda's shocked expression. She touched the control button on the phone and spoke again "Show me the technical specs for a Viridian Seven series Companion. Specifically the mental capacity and hardware."

The phone took a second to complete this request, producing a list of links. One of them was a video, titled "What's inside a Viridian Seven series?" Sasha tapped it and it began to play.

A rather nerdy looking young man with a very obvious ocular implant appeared and began gushing about the technological marvel that was the Viridian Seven series. Sasha fast forwarded a bit, until the man stood and a blond-haired version of Amanda stepped into frame, a vacant smile on her face. Amanda leaned forward and said "Volume up." The video grew louder.

"This is Sarah, my own personal Seven series. Now, Sarah means a lot to me, so I'm not going to be taking her apart for this, but I also have Rebecca here," he reached below the desk he had been seated at and produced a severed head. Amanda recoiled as a jolt of fright ran through her. This one had longer hair than Amanda, but it was dark, with pink stripes, and it struck very close to home. The eyes were clouded over in a film and the flesh was pallid.

"Rebecca, unfortunately, was involved in an accident at the spaceport, and her biological components were damaged beyond repair. Fun fact: the vat-grown tissue which the Viridian Seven series uses means that any damage to any part of her body can be treated medically, just like a person! Unfortunately, that also means that once senescence sets in, there's nothing we can do.

"Now, Rebecca here was given to me by her owner once the extent of the damage was known. I didn't have much use for the rest, so I got rid of it. It's unpleasant, truth be told. I kind of felt like a serial killer, disposing of one of my victims." The video footage went grainy and dark and spooky music played for a second as it zoomed in on his face. After a moment, it returned to normal and he continued speaking. "And after this video, I'll be removing the rest of the biological matter from her computer, so that I can order a new body and have it implanted. The bodies themselves aren't actually that expensive;

most of the costs go into what's here." He tapped the side of the head for the camera, then turned the head to face himself and grimaced at it. He turned it towards the vacant-eyed sex-bot seated to his left. "What do you think, Sarah?"

"I think it's good that you're going to help Rebecca get a new body!" the bot said in a bright and chipper voice, without once taking her eyes off the camera. Amanda felt like she could see stress and fear in the bot's eyes, but the canned response suggested that it might just be her imagination.

Sasha looked at Amanda, "That's not your voice," she said, "yours is a little deeper and huskier." Amanda tried to flash a smile at her, but it was difficult to do, given what she was watching. Sasha's eyebrows turned up in a sympathetic tilt and she put an arm around Amanda's shoulder. Amanda leaned into her and continued watching.

"Okay, so we've got to get through the skull here." He picked up a razor and used it to cut through the flesh of the scalp, from the top of the head all the way to the base of the skull. Amanda felt her gorge rise as he grabbed at the scalp and yanked hard several times to separate it from the skull beneath. She clenched her teeth tightly and willed her stomach to settle as the young man used a power cutting tool to cut around the entire back of the skull. He continued to prattle on to the camera genially, but Amanda wasn't listening. The sight of him cutting through the skull was morbidly fascinating, filling Amanda with a hollow, cold feeling. He managed to finally get the chunk he'd cut free loose, and drew it away with a flourish and a zoom-in of the camera.

The inside was free of blood or other fluids, except for a few tiny smears from his fingers. As the man cleaned his hands off-screen, Amanda looked at the circuitry and hardware inside the skull.

"Is that what the inside of my head looks like?" she asked.

"No!" Sasha said, letting go of Amanda to retrieve her neural imager. She tapped the screen for a moment, then said "render" and stared at it. When she turned it towards Amanda, a 3d object rotated slowly on the screen. "Well, I mean, some of the parts look the same, but the overall configuration is very different. Look; the hardware in your head is an entirely different shape. You've got a lot more of it, too. Look how much empty space there is in the video. Your head is mostly packed, and you've got lipids between components, like padding or something. And like he said at the beginning, the DNA samples the clonal tissue is based on came from humans right here on Arthesia. You have that bot's face, but you are very, very different."

"So we're right back to it being a mystery, then."

"No, this doesn't change anything. If you got injured while in a virtual environment, you might have needed to replace more than your brain. And there's still a chance you're from one of the Digital Arcologies. Either way, you might have just picked a new face from a bunch of choices that included the Seven series. Or... " Sasha paused and eyed her.

"Or what?"

"Or maybe you work for Viridian Dynamics! If you were a high-enough ranked executive, you'd have the sway to model the Series seven after yourself, and given all the high-tech stuff they have fingers in, you'd have plenty of opportunity to be logged into a neural-simulating virtual environment, too. So maybe *they* look like *you*." Sasha nodded to herself, clearly pleased with her new theory. "I've changed my mind. I think that's what happened."

"So you think I'm a high-level executive at Viridian Dynamics? Then how did I end up dating a street kid like Mike?"

The thought of Mike raised a tide of guilt. She had jumped into bed with Sasha, never considering that she might be hurting someone in doing so. She shoved it back down. That was a problem for another time.

Sasha frowned, but only for a second. "Maybe you were slumming it. Didn't you tell me that Mike had just gotten some big new job with a government contractor? Well, Viridian is a government contractor. One of the biggest. Maybe you guys met at work and you decided to have a fling with a bad boy."

Amanda thought about that. Sasha made a lot of sense. Given the way she'd almost thrown herself at Sasha last night, and the ease with which she'd negotiated with the homeless man the night before, she suspected she was probably pretty adventurous before she lost her memory. She pictured herself as a high-powered executive who happened to come across an up-jumped street tough. It made sense, but… There was another explanation.

She might just be a sex-bot.

The fact that her genome was Draughtgen, or that the hardware in her head didn't match the dead bot on Sasha's phone didn't eliminate that possibility. She might be custom-built, or a different model. One that Viridian kept secret. So what would be the purpose of building a sex-bot with a Draughtgen body? Well, it could survive a lot of abuse.

Among the scraps of memory she had held onto through whatever had happened to her were a few brief flashes that had terrified her. She'd avoided thinking about them so far, but she forced herself to review them, now.

Rough hands squeezing her throat while a man shoved his penis into her mouth in a sudden, brutal thrust, laughing as she gagged and struggled. Her ankles, bound so tightly to a rope around her waist that pain shot through her legs as a woman laid into her crotch mercilessly with a riding crop. Needles being shoved through her skin as she squirmed against bonds that held her tightly. Amanda remembered what it was like to have her lips sewn shut around a feeding tube. She couldn't put that sensation into any sort of context, but she remembered the sensation and the knowledge of what caused it. She knew what it felt like to have electrodes connected to nipples, labia and other sensitive areas. She remembered the sharp pain of whips striking her legs and back, the burning itch of razors slicing her flesh.

As an explanation for her body, that was certainly simpler. But there were problems with that possibility, as well. There were facts that didn't fit. The way she'd felt when Mike appeared on the security camera footage at the jewelry shop. Comfort. Joy. Happiness. Not the cold, empty dread that gnawed at her heart as she relived those flashes.

She could not accept that Mike had been her abuser. A rescuer, maybe. Perhaps he'd taken her away from whoever left her with those horrible memories.

And her Behavioral State codes. The idea of taking a sex-bot, built to be raped and abused, and teaching it to kill without hesitation was, well... Nonsensical, to put it mildly. No-one would want a torture doll that would kill them if they went too far.

Unless the owner wasn't supposed to know. Such a bot would then have a very useful purpose; an assassin. She pictured herself suffering under some CEO or government official, snapping and turning violent. She pictured herself beating him to death and leaping out a window, naked, covered in bruises. But then, why allow such horrible memories to form in the first place? Why not kill him the moment they were alone.

Perhaps those memories didn't tell her anything about her purpose. She didn't have to be built to survive abuse. She remembered Sasha's prescription bottle. Plenty of people survived abuse, and she was sure that a normal human could survive the things she remembered.

They might be just something she'd experienced, which had made a predictably deep impact on her. They might be memories of an old boyfriend, abusive and sadistic. They might be her own masochistic fantasies, fulfilled. They might have been anything; hell, they might have been the 'accident' in Sasha's theory. She didn't know how her mind might have survived intact, but then, she didn't really know that it had, did she?

Perhaps whatever put her into that alley hadn't been her first brush with losing herself.

But then, who was David? She pictured him, barbed wire tattoo and muscular arms. Handsome and dangerous, like a street tough from a film. She remembered the shield he'd had. He had planned to be shot at, though he apparently hadn't planned to shoot back. He was some sort of investigator or possibly a spy.

Which meant she might be a spy. But spies generally didn't need to fight, because a spy who found themselves in a fight was a failed spy. Amanda wasn't sure where that pithy-sounding statement had come from, but she felt like it contained some truth.

There were so many pieces. Her unusual mix of hardware and biology. Extreme toughness and the ability to fight. Other state codes that spoke to other abilities. Honeypots and tradecrafts and the ominous 'contagion'. Mike and the warm feelings he evoked in her. David and his shady importance. But putting them all together into a coherent whole was too difficult. For all the pieces of the puzzle she had, she was still missing too many to make sense of it all.

A sex-bot for sadists. A combat bot. An assassin bot. A spy-bot. Or a corporate executive. One of these things was not like the other, but honestly, she couldn't rule out any of them. She just didn't know enough. She didn't have enough pieces.

She needed to gather more. She needed some time to use her BCI and do some more research.

Sasha seemed to read her mind, because she said "Are you hungry? There's a place a couple blocks away with the best beef noodles and pineapple buns."

Amanda smiled, "Do you think you could get it? I need to use my BCI and do some research. I really appreciate how helpful you've been, but I still need to look a lot of stuff up, now."

"Sure, no problem. Let me get dressed, and I'll be back in half an hour. You can stay naked." Sasha grinned and eyed her up and down. "You *should* stay naked."

Amanda smiled back. She had other things on her mind right now, but maybe after they ate…

"I probably will. I'll be right here, just thinking at one of the computers in my head."

Sasha climbed out of the bed and dressed quickly while Amanda looked up Draughtgen on her BCI, displaying reference text from what she thought might be the most reliable sites in the center of her vision, where it was easy to read.

Once she had clothes and shoes on, Sasha grabbed her phone and headed towards the living room. She stopped in the doorway and looked back, a worried expression on her face.

"You're going to be here when I get back, right?"

Amanda dismissed the image in front of her and met Sasha's gaze. "Of course, why wouldn't I be?"

"Well, it's just… This whole thing with you, it's like something out of a movie. And if this was a movie, then you'd be gone when I got back, and I'd find a note saying that you had a great time, but staying here would be putting me in danger. And then you'd turn back up in a couple of days, all beat to hell and I'd help you and we'd have one more night together before some bad guys showed up and kidnapped us both and then they'd kill me while you watched and you'd get so mad that when you broke free you'd kill them all. And I don't mind the thought that me dying would make you that angry, but, like… I don't wanna die."

Amanda tilted her head to the side in amusement. "This isn't a movie, hun. And besides, I've already shown up beaten to hell and back, and you helped me, and we had a wonderful night. And look! No kidnappers."

Sasha smiled a little tentatively, but Amanda could see the desperate hope there. "Okay. I'll be back in thirty minutes, tops." She turned, and Amanda pinched her behind, for good measure.

When she heard the front door close, she sat back down. Even with Amanda's surprisingly deep attraction to the woman, Sasha's behavior seemed… Odd. She looked around the room, taking in the mess. Books, tablets and clothes were scattered everywhere. But there were clear piles, and a sort of pattern. There was a book on gardening on the windowsill, next to a small potted plant that seemed to be thriving. One stack of books and tablets on the desk had the word "anatomy" in every visible title. She checked one of the tablets, and sure enough, it contained a work on anatomy. Another stack was about drugs. A third was about genetics.

There was order in the chaos here. Amanda poked through Sasha's closet. Her fashion was eccentric, eye-catching and dramatic. Bright pinks and blacks were equally represented, and they dominated the color scheme, which was rounded out with blood reds and deep purples. At one end, Amanda found a full, Victorian formal gown done in black with pink trim. Ravens and skulls dominated the extensive threadwork.

Amanda considered what all of this told her about Sasha. Her clothes demanded attention, possibly meaning she didn't get enough attention as-is. The organized chaos in the room suggested a sharp, but easily distracted mind. Attention-deficit, or possibly on the autism spectrum.

There was an answer there, floating in the cloud of facts. It was so obvious that it seemed almost wrong to consider it, but Amanda tried, anyway. Maybe Sasha was an outcast. A social pariah of sorts. Possibly the result of whatever incident had led to her needing emergency contraceptives at such a young age. Amanda had come to her needing help, and Sasha had glommed on to her with a fervor borne of desperation. Desperation which was, itself, borne of a life of loneliness.

It made sense, and no other answers really fit everything. The question was, was that a threat?

Amanda had no idea. She didn't even know how to try to answer the question. Until she remembered the behavioral state codes. One of them had mentioned 'tradecraft', which she was pretty sure meant 'spycraft'. A spy would have experience evaluating people, analyzing them for threats and weaknesses.

She sat down on the bed, taking deep breaths. She hoped this wouldn't backfire on her.

Orchid

The complexities immediately became workable.

The obvious answer was most likely correct, and Sasha was most likely not a threat. Her social anxieties were the self-fulfilling cause of her obvious social isolation, which Sasha compensated for with the attention-grabbing wardrobe. Amanda shook her head in self-disgust that she hadn't even bothered to consider how Sasha's nervous chatter fitted into the picture before now. High intelligence, social anxieties, loneliness and the fact that she hadn't exhibited any overtly toxic traits associated with ideologies who recruited such people, it all pointed in a single direction. It wasn't even a difficult puzzle. Sasha was, for lack of a better term, a mere introverted nerd. She'd latched onto Amanda as both an exciting puzzle and an attractive woman, and Amanda's casual acceptance, borne both of necessity and her own inexplicable attraction to the woman had only encouraged her. The sense of familiarity she felt with Sasha was, itself, a red flag, but it stood alone. Reality was often like that. Answers weren't always clear, even when they were true.

Sasha was smart, had useful medical knowledge, and -another detail she hadn't bothered to notice before- Sasha seemed to be quite physically fit. Amanda recalled the muscles moving under Sasha's skin last night with a clinical detachment, recognizing the distinctive build of a gym rat. And her ears… They weren't as misshapen as those of the boy who'd caught her eye, peering out of the alley. But there were lumps and knots there. A martial artist, too. An activity that didn't suit the rest of her personality, except that it put her in regular contact with people. A reprieve from her social isolation.

Evaluation: Not a threat. And she could be very useful as an ally.

`Daisy`

The sense of detached coldness flowed away. She breathed a sigh of relief and resolved to run with it. Sasha very clearly had attachment issues, but the results of her behavior lined up with Amanda's goals, as well as aligning with Amanda's own need to have *someone* in her own life that she could rely on.

And there was just something about Sasha that spoke to her. She had felt the first, subtle tinges of it in the store, yesterday. She'd felt it much more strongly in the car and here, last night. There was something about Sasha that told Amanda that she could be trusted. That she could be relied upon.

True to her word, Sasha returned in a half-hour. She opened the front door to find Amanda, still undressed, sitting on the couch, staring off into space. She let out a laugh that was ninety percent relieved tension and Amanda stood to help her carry the two bags and a drink carrier with a couple steaming cups of coffee in it.

"I left some money on your coffee table to cover mine, I hope twenty is enough." Sasha laughed again, a more humored sound this time. "Keep your money! I paid nineteen for the whole meal." Sasha removed a few textbooks from the tiny table in the kitchen and they took seats.

True to Sasha's word, the beef noodles and pineapple buns were amazing. While they ate, Amanda explained to Sasha what she'd been thinking about and what she'd learned.

She shared with Sasha her suspicions about her origins. How she might be a sex-bot for sadists or an assassin. How she might be a masochist who took things too far one time. Or how she might be caught up in something bigger.

"The first thing I looked for was political assassinations. And I found one that I thought might be me. Look," Amanda sent a video she'd found; a news report to Sasha's phone. In it, the reporter discussed the assasination of Generals Covington and Chau, last year. The assassinations that had ended the military Junta that once controlled the People's Republic of Arthesia, leaving a void filled by the militia. A sex worker, brought into the capitol compound by General Chau had killed him, the Prime Minister General Covington, Covington's wife and several guards. Even one of the Prime Minister's young sons had been wounded in the hit.

She'd watched that news report, her excitement growing, until they finally showed a picture of the attacker, a still from the security footage. Certainty gave way to confusion. Because it clearly wasn't Amanda. The woman in the 3d image was short and whipcord thin, her limbs wrapped in tight, dense muscles. Her face was different, pockmarked with the remains of teenage acne. Her eyes were hard and sharp, soulless and deep.

"That one really had me going, but it wasn't the only one. I found news reports about thirty more assassinations. I narrowed it down to eight; all of them suspect a woman, and none had a description that didn't rule me out. But that's where I hit a wall, so I gave following that idea and started researching Viridian and these sex-bots that look like me. That was easy to find information on, because Viridian's been in the news a lot for the past decade or so.

"I found out that Viridian made their original sex-bots out of silicone and and other synthetic materials and they had these, sort of, serial numbers. The last line was the MX-50s, which was a significant upgrade over the MX-40 line, because they used military-grade computers to make them more lifelike, make them act like girlfriends, instead of sexbots.

"It's weird, because a lot of the stuff I read about them doesn't seem appealing. They can start arguments, get moody, develop likes and dislikes that the owner can't control, stuff like that. But they were a huge hit. Viridian sold enough of them to fund the research into the clonal tissue construction process that they used to make the Series fives. There were no Series one through four; I guess it's a marketing thing or something.

"They really tout this clonal tissue construction thing. It's a trade secret that they say lets them build a Series seven body in two days. It's supposed to be a lot cheaper than the old way of building them, too. So the Series five and on cost about half as much as the prior models. About half of their ad campaign touts how real the tissue is. The other half touts how real the bots themselves behave.

"Another thing is, as it turns out, Viridian has a connection to the Draughtgen. They have an employee from there, they hired her twenty years back. About fifteen years ago, a Viridian Security Services group headed up by this woman tried to do some recruiting among Imperial Defense Force vets, apparently hoping to be able to field a unit of Draughtgen mercenaries. They pretty much failed, though. I guess the Draughtgen didn't like the idea of becoming mercenaries or something, but in the end, they only signed three contracts.

"Since three people aren't enough to make an effective field team, they made them middle management and gave them desk jobs. All three immediately sued to get out of the contract, citing the change in terms, and surprisingly; Viridian just accepted it. Cut them big severance checks, had them sign NDA's and shipped them right back home. For all the trouble they went to, for all their expense in recruiting those three, they just kinda shrugged and moved on. Which isn't what I'd expect from a big corporation like that.

"The original one, though… I couldn't find any solid information on her. Which makes no sense, really. Viridian had been touting her in their recruitment campaigns, hoping it would convince more to sign on. So I found her name and picture easily enough on their recruiting ads, but aside from some obviously scripted quotes about how much she enjoys working for Viridian, there's almost *no* information on her out there.

"The company's website lists her as a 'Special Developments Consultant' and has her picture and her resume there, but there's nothing about what she does for the company, or even where she is. Before Viridian snatched her up, she worked in, get this, clonal tissue production. For a medical company in the Empire. Sure enough, about five years after she started is when the Series five premiered. Right before their headhunting expedition in the Empire."

"So you've seen her picture?" Sasha raised her eyebrows and Amanda understood the implicit question there. "Yes," she answered, "It's not me." She transmitted a photo from her BCI to Sasha's phone.

Sasha picked up her phone and looked. The face staring back at her was longer, with more angular features and close-cropped, brown hair. Her eyes were gray, cold and hard, nothing like Amanda's expressive baby-blues.

"So not you. That's a little disappointing, but it doesn't really mean anything. Well, except that you're not, uh, Rachel Hornsby. Wow, what a name."

"Yeah," Amanda said, pausing to stuff an entire pineapple bun in her mouth and chew it up. When she got it down, she continued. "So then I started splitting the difference, looking into deaths involving Viridian. And that's when I found this."

This time, she willed her BCI to share the link directly with Sasha's phone. Sasha glanced down as the screen changed and began to read.

Shooting At Viridian Dynamics Head Office

Saturday, December 26th. Violence broke out at the Viridian Dynamics headquarters, today. At about 2:40 PM local time, witnesses reported gunfire and screaming coming from the lobby of the Viridian Dynamics headquarters building in New Kowloon. Police rushed to the scene, but before they arrived, witnesses reported several individuals fleeing in what appeared to be a vehicle pursuit.

On the scene, I spoke to Bob Kun, owner of the Sunny Day Cheer Cafe, right across the street from the iconic corporate building.

"I called the cops when I heard the shooting, and the man I spoke to said they'd already gotten other calls and patrol bots were on their way. So I just watched out the front window, you know? I tried to keep still, because I don't know if somebody wants to get rid of any witnesses or anything. Anyways, I see two people run out the front, a man and a woman, all covered in blood and carrying guns. They're running out, and the woman is shooting over her shoulder with a gun. They ran up to this car that was just sitting there and jump in the back, and the car takes off like [squealing tire sounds].

"Anyways, right as they jumped in, a bunch of guys, some of them in suits and the rest of them looking like gang members run out after them, just shooting like there's no tomorrow. Bullets are going everywhere, you can see the holes in my window where they shot through it. Anyways, the first group took off, so the second group goes running to a bunch of SUVs and a flier and they all hop in and take off after them. I don't know why anyone was shooting at anyone else, but that's what I saw. The patrol bots got here right after and most of 'em rushed inside, but a couple came out to see if anyone was hurt out here. The one comes in here and asks me if I'm okay, and I tell him I am, and then he left. And that's all that happened until you guys got here."

According to police, the shooting left six Viridian Dynamics employees dead. Four more employees were reported missing, after failing to come into work or call. Police attempted to contact them, but received no response. So far, there's no word on who the shooters might be. After speaking to Mr. Kun, I managed to get a moment with Police Detective Gardner, who said "Right now, we don't know if the two unknown individuals are responsible for the deaths inside, and the evidence is unclear enough that I won't speculate. We're working on pulling the security footage now. We'll know more tomorrow."

Local workers and the residents of the nearby White Flower residential building have been shaken by these events…

Sasha put it down after reading the important bits. "Wow. So you think maybe you were that woman?"

"Maybe," Amanda shrugged, "And Maybe Mike was the man? Or maybe I'm one of the missing employees, or maybe what happened to me has nothing at all to do with this, or maybe I don't even have anything to do with Viridian." She sighed, finishing her coffee and slumping back in her seat. "I just don't know. Every time it seems like I might find an answer, all I find are even more questions."

Sasha finished her own coffee and stood. She walked around behind Amanda and hugged her. "We'll figure this out. I'm sure of it."

"We, huh?" Amanda smiled at her to make sure she knew she wasn't trying to push the other woman away. "Well, duh," Sasha said. "As long as I'm not gonna get fridged, I'm gonna help. And even if I am gonna get fridged, as long as you promise to avenge me, I'll have your back."

Amanda nodded in faux seriousness, "I promise, if you get killed to motivate me to solve this mystery, I'll murder my way through whoever's responsible. Speaking of which, know where I can get some more guns? I've only got the one…"

Sasha stood up straight and crooked her arms, flexing a pair of impressive biceps. "Boom, boom," she said, "Firepower." Amanda laughed helplessly at the silliness and Sasha grinned back, proud of her joke. Amanda eyed her, that same vague sense of familiarity and comfort returning, stirring other feelings in its wake. Her mind turned away from the mystery before them.

"Well," Amanda said, "It's good to know I'm already at the gun shop," She stood and turned, putting her hands on Sasha's waist and pulling her in. Sasha didn't resist. "Damn straight," she said, "I mean, I've never actually been in a street fight, but

I've been lifting weights and doing MMA since I was sixteen. I could knock a motherfucker out."

"Hmm, I wonder if you could crush a man's head between your thighs."

Sasha wiggled her knees a little, "Maybe," she said, running her hands up and down Amanda's sides.

"I wonder if you could crush mine," Amanda said, and nudged Sasha's nose with her own.

"Well," Sasha said philosophically. "There's only one way to find out."

Active

"Not that I'm not having the time of my life," Amanda said an hour later as they lay in bed, catching their breath, "But I'm going to have to get moving. I know there's a lead on where Mike is, if I can just find out where Debra Chan's cousin's daughter lives. The man at the first jewelry store I went to seemed to know Debra Chan, maybe he'll know her cousin. I need to head over there and find out."

Sasha groaned, then stretched. Amanda watched her body move in the light streaming in through the windows and fought off a little surprise that someone so insecure could live in such a powerful body.

"Give me a minute to get dressed. Like, really dressed, not just throwing something on like I did to run out for breakfast. I'll drive you."

"You don't have to-"

"Don't say that!" Amanda shut her mouth at the sudden exclamation. "I want to."

"Okay. Thank you, Sasha. You've been so wonderful to me, I don't know how to repay you."

"Just... Just let me tag along and help you figure this out. And then, maybe consider if, maybe, you might like to have a girlfriend, a little..."

Amanda smiled at her, but Sasha wasn't done. Stress had overtaken her features and pulled them into a worried frown, and she'd gone into a full ramble. "I mean, I know we just met, and it's suuuuuper weird for me to talking about, like, going steady and stuff, but, I dunno, I just get a really good vibe from you, and you're so cool and sweet, and…" She paused and her frown deepened into a self-recriminating grimace, "And I just realized that I don't even know if you have a girlfriend, or a boy- Oh my god, Mike was your boyfriend, wasn't he? I'm such an idiot, god, forget I said anything, I'm so stupid, I-"

"Sasha!" Amanda yelled, startling the other woman out of her self-recriminating fugue.

"Huh?"

"Relax, hon! Look, I need to find Mike. And yes, there was something there. You know I can't make any promises right now. I feel like Mike is someone very special to me. Maybe he's the one my heart belongs to. But you are special, too. I haven't even known you a single day, but I feel like I've known you my whole life. You're beautiful, you've been so helpful, and I think you're very charming." Amanda smiled at Sasha, who smiled back tentatively.

"What I can promise you is that you mean a lot to me. No matter what, I want to be your friend. And if it's at all possible, I would love to be more than that."

Sasha brightened a little. "You really mean that?"

"Yes, really," Amanda kissed her, licking her lips lightly. "Now go get dressed. I've got to get dressed, too."

Sasha bounced out of bed and began chattering about colors while Amanda walked out to the living room. She looked at her clothes. They were torn and covered in blood and dirt. "Sasha," she called, "Do you have a washing machine?"

"Yeah it's…" Sasha walked out of the room, a pair of panties in her hand, then stopped.

"Oh, right, your clothes! Yeah, you can't wear those. They're ruined. Come on, I've got plenty of smart fabric stuff that'll size itself to you." Amanda grabbed her clutch and retrieved the panties and socks from within it before turning to follow Sasha back into the bedroom. She was running low, already.

They spent probably longer than they should picking out clothes, but Amanda found the exercise enjoyable. It was nice to have something that wasn't a mystery or just horrifyingly violent to focus on.

Eventually, they settled on pants and blouses with jackets. They were the most practical outfits Sasha had, but even then, everything was decorated and rhinestoned and glittery. Amanda's shirt was hot pink, with a bright red pair of lips across the front, and a smaller pair with an arrow pointing down on the back. She put it on backwards at first, getting a laugh out of Sasha. "Obey the shirt," Amanda joked in somber tones, which almost led to the undoing of their progress getting dressed.

Her jacket was black leather, but was bespeckled with glittering rhinestones in a tasteful pattern across it. For pants, she chose a pair of what Sasha called 'fuck me jeans', which looked baggy and loose at first, but tightened up significantly as she pulled them on, until she could see she had a crease in the front, as well as the back. She asked how to loosen them, but Sasha just shrugged. A few tentative kicks convinced her that they wouldn't be a problem if she tried to run, so she shrugged and left them on. Sasha's description was accurate, she thought. She could almost get fucked while wearing them, they were so tight and flexible.

She got her stolen boots and a pair of socks on, and thought they were ready to go. "I need to do my makeup," Sasha said, and Amanda paused, realizing that she should do the same. They both crowded into the tiny bathroom and used Sasha's copious collection to doll themselves up. Amanda did essentially the same thing she'd done the day before, but used a darker and less saturated shade of lipstick, to better match her jacket.

Finally done, they left. Sasha drove like a maniac while Amanda held on for dear life and fed her directions. It took less than five minutes to arrive, and another twenty five minutes to find a parking spot. They ended up parking three blocks away.

Everything inside the shop looked the same, except there was a young woman sitting behind the counter. "Um, excuse me, the man who was here yesterday, is he around?"

The young woman smiled at her, "Yeah, just a second." She put down a tablet she'd been reading and stepped further back into the shop. A second later, her voice rang out loudly. "DAD! You've got customers!'

Amanda and Sasha both jerked at the sudden shout, and then caught each other's eye and giggled. A moment later, Marcus stepped out from where the young lady had gone. The woman was right behind him. She took her seat back and picked up the tablet, her attention fully absorbed.

Marcus stopped when he saw Amanda. His mouth opened for a second, then closed. After another second or two, he spoke, sounding nervous. "Uh, perhaps you'd like to speak in the back? I'm sure there's no reason to disturb her studies…"

Amanda nodded, "That's fine," she said and both women followed him.

He led them back through a hall whose walls braced large stacks of boxes. The whole rear of the shop smelled of metal and chemicals, and it was dusty and none-too-tidy. It felt like a place in which a lot of careful work was done, but not a lot of care given to the space itself.

He opened a narrow wooden door to reveal a surprisingly spacious office. It was sparsely decorated, with nothing but a few professional certifications on the wall. He gestured to a small table that occupied the wall opposite a cluttered desk, and all three sat down.

"Before we conduct any business," Marcus said as soon as their butts had touched the seats, "I need to know if you were involved with what happened to Miss Chan."

Amanda stared at him for a second. She had been hoping he hadn't heard about the attack, but of course, that was mere wishful thinking. It had probably made the news within hours, and rumors always moved faster than the news, in any event.

"I was there when it happened," she admitted. "Another customer had come in after me, and Debrah was just closing up for the day. She was going to help me out with… With something else when she was done. So this guy came in, and they started talking, and then the next thing I know, the glass was shattering and there were bullets and blood everywhere." She paused, taking a deep shuddering breath, not needing to fake her emotional reaction one bit.

"The guy who came in after me, he grabbed me and pushed me out the back, and then offered to let me come with him. I think the people shooting were there for him, because they started chasing us. Things got hectic, and I fell out of the car."

"You fell out of the-" Marcus exclaimed before cutting himself off. He composed his features and asked "Have you spoken to the police yet? They're looking for you, you know. They called here, asking about you."

"They did?" Amanda gasped and Sasha looked worried.

"They did. They called yesterday evening, and then again this morning. The detective I spoke to both times asked if I'd seen a Viridian Seven series with black hair with red stripes dyed in it. I told her that I had not, because as I said yesterday, it is clear that you simply bear a strong resemblance to the Seven series."

"You… You lied to them?"

"Young lady, the cops lie to us all. It's only fair to return the favor." Marcus fixed her with a hard look. "But you should explain quickly why I shouldn't ask both of you to leave right now. I may not like the police, but I have no interest in getting caught up in whatever this is. And no compunction about calling them to remove troublemakers."

Amanda nodded. "It's the thing Miss Chan was going to help me with. Her cousin's daughter lives with a man I need to speak to. She was going to take me there, but she never got the chance to do it before they… They killed her. I need to speak to this man, it's very important."

Marcus looked back and forth between the two of them slowly, evaluating Amanda's words. A long moment stretched out as the gears in his head turned. Finally, he spoke.

"I know Miss Chan's cousin. Emilia Codswell. I can give you her address. She would know where to find her daughter and this man you need to speak to."

"Please!" Amanda said, relieved to hear it, "It would mean so much to me. I just need her address, and then we'll go, and I promise not to get you involved in anything."

Marcus nodded, then stood and walked over to the desk. He cleared away some papers from a built-in console and tapped the screen a couple of times. "What's your phone's name?"

Amanda thought.

`CompanionAssist-7218.`

Well, shit, that wasn't going to work. The man had already mistaken her for a sex-bot, having a BCI with that name would only arouse his suspicion. *Can I change it?* She thought at her BCI.

Please choose a new name now.

Amanda's Phone, she thought.

Confirmed. New device name is Amanda's Phone.

"Amanda's phone," she said. The man tapped the screen again, and an address popped up in her field of view.

"Thank you," she said, standing up. Sasha followed her, still quiet. "Thank you very much, you don't know how much this means to me..." She quickly hugged him and then moved to leave.

"Wait!" he said.

Amanda turned back, a question on her face. Marcus's features had softened, and he looked upset. His eyes had a pleading look to them. Amanda supposed it was over what had happened to Miss Chan. When he spoke, he confirmed it.

"Do you still have those earrings? I'd... I don't own anything Miss Chan made. And she was such a fixture in the industry here, that I'd really like to own something to remember her by. I... I can pay you the full price for them. Not the six thousand we agreed on."

"Um, are you sure?"

"Yes, I'm quite sure. If you still have them, that is."

"I do, I just... Well, okay. Sure."

Marcus nodded and gestured for them to lead the way back to the front.

"How would you like to accept payment? I can do a debit transfer, or PayMate, or-"

"Cash," Amanda said. Marcus' eyes widened. "I'm not sure I have that much at hand, are you sure?"

Amanda wracked her brain for any other option. If she had a bank account, she didn't know about it.

    The   CompanionAssist   includes   a
Financial   Ministry   approved   digital
wallet   capable   of   conducting
transactions of up to $2,168,212 and
storing   balances   of   up   to
$6,000,000,000.

How would I transfer money into it? She questioned.

    Debit transfer.

She spoke up, "Okay. I'll take a debit transfer, then."

"Good, good. Just a moment, then." Marcus tapped on the till for a second, then looked up.

"If you'll just give me your 'print, here…" He pointed to a thumbprint scanner.

Amanda placed her thumb on the scanner, and a notification popped up in her field of view. She jerked in surprise.

"Eighty five hundred!?" Amanda gasped.

"I, well, threw a little extra in. I suspect you might need it. Consider it a 'thank you' for the rapid conclusion of our business here."

Amanda caught the hint.

"Yes, thank you. Thank you so much, you've been so helpful!" She leaned over the counter and squeezed him tightly. He looked very uncomfortable, so she broke it off quickly and dug into her purse to hand over the earrings.

She looked back as they were walking out the door to see the young woman shaking her head sadly at her father, though her lips were curled in a little smile.

As soon as the door closed, Sasha spoke "That was easy. And helpful, too!"

Amanda nodded, feeling a little overwhelmed by the man's help. "I can hardly believe it. It's like everyone I meet either wants to kill me or help me."

Sasha smiled. "It's because you're so pretty. And sweet."

Amanda blushed. "I doubt that. I'm all beat up and bruised…" Sasha stopped and grabbed her arm. "No, you're not."

She pointed at the window of the shop they were standing in front of. Amanda looked, letting her eyes focus on her reflection there. The bruises that had marred her features last night were gone. She touched her skin experimentally, and it felt perfectly normal. She suddenly remember putting her makeup on, and recalled an image of her face then. Her BCi helpfully pulled up a recording of what she'd been seeing, and she noted some thin, yellow bruising that was not in evidence in her reflection.

She twisted her back experimentally. The pain, from both her lower back and upper back was nothing in comparison to how it felt the previous night. A lot more of a dull ache than the hot, stabbing pain it had been.

"I'm healing really fast," she said.

"Yeah. You're chock full of medical systems. There's at least forty different types of nanites in your bloodstream. I thought most of them were compatibility stuff; you know, letting the hardware in your head properly interface with your body, but after we got up this morning, I noticed that almost all of your bruising was gone."

Amanda stared at her own reflection for a few more minutes, wondering how this fit in. Sasha hadn't mentioned this before, but that really didn't mean much. Did it? Amanda got the impression that it hadn't surprised Sasha. But it was quite a surprise to her. Sasha's words about finding medical nanites provided a ready explanation, though. She hadn't been surprised, because she'd known about the nanites. She just hadn't known what they did until that morning.

It didn't change anything, really. The presence of medical systems was exactly the sort of thing they'd put in a combat bot with organic components.

But why a combat robot? If she was a designer of some sort, or a senior executive, why wouldn't she have had a body just like her original one built?

Amanda pulled back up the photo of Rachel Hornsby. She studied it for a long time. Draughtgen. Combat veteran. Security expert. Exactly the sort of person who might pick a combat bot model to replace her body after a catastrophic accident.

Inspiration struck. "Sasha, I think I might actually be Rachel Hornsby. The photo we looked at, that could be my original body. She's exactly the kind of person who would pick a combat bot body to replace her own, right? She's a security expert and a combat veteran, and a Draughtgen. Maybe Viridian just didn't update the photo after the accident."

Sasha frowned. "I don't know…" She thought for a moment, and then her face lit up in inspiration. "Rachel was a big deal for Viridian. If Rachel had an accident, they wouldn't have covered it up; they'd have wanted to keep her happy, so they'd be open about it and make a big show of helping her in every way they can."

"Still," Amanda said, "We can rule it out just by calling Viridian and asking to speak to her. If she answers or if they can get us contact info on her, we'd know it's not me. If she's unavailable, then we can search for more proof."

"I don't think that's a good idea," Sasha said. "I don't trust Viridian, and we don't know who those guys who snatched you are. For all we know, they're working for Viridian, and calling and asking to speak to Rachel will set them after us."

Amanda frowned. She was sure there was something they could do to protect themselves if Viridian sent people. Just moving away from the place they had called from would do it. But, she thought with a sigh, Sasha seemed dead set against it. She didn't want to drive a wedge between them. She decided to table the idea for now. They could always try later on, when they'd run out of other options. For now, they had a lead on Ming.

Manyan province was an entirely different world from the rest of New Kowloon. Amanda had grown used to the narrow streets that alternated between worn-but-clean and filthy-and-run-down, the dense crowds, the inescapable smells of garbage and food and sweat. Every building and vehicle was either ancient or brand new, with a heavy skew towards the ancient. Outside of the commercial areas, the smiling, well-dressed people Amanda had noticed had been nowhere to be seen.

Even the neighborhood Sasha lived in fit the theme. The streets were clean, but narrow, and full of filled-in potholes. The buildings crowded in on each other like they did everywhere else, though the almost ever-present graffiti elsewhere was missing.

But Manyan province was something else. The streets were broad, and lacked sidewalks. Sculpted topiary lined the roads, and the buildings were all separated by expanses of green grass and meticulously manicured gardens. The buildings were all of an indiscernible age; they might have been well-maintained and a century old, or brand new and antiqued to give them that 'old-money' feel. Her BCI informed her that none of these buildings were actually a century old, as Manyan province had been a slum until it underwent a drastic gentrification process, decades ago.

Sasha seemed unphased by the ostentatious display of wealth. They'd had to pass through three checkpoints to get here, and even those hadn't bothered her. She'd pulled over and taken Amanda's gun, hiding it somewhere in the undercarriage of the car. Then she'd driven right up, smiling and flirting awkwardly with the cops checking IDs.

Amanda had decided to leave the gun where it was, not expecting to have to use it to talk to Ming and Miss Chan's relative. She recalled and shared with Sasha the warning that she'd gotten. "Miss Chan's cousin and her husband have security who will get very violent, so we need to make sure to find the entrance to the guests house and stay there."

They found the address easily enough; between Amanda's BCI feeding her directions and the fact that there were never more than two or three addresses on a block, they quickly found it. It was a massive, walled compound on several acres. The front contained an ornate gate, set back several dozen feet from the road. Large shishi statues stood on either side of the entrance, guarding the way. Small electrical boxes at the base of the statues indicated that they were packed full of electronics. Probably security stuff.

They drove around. There were two other entrances. The first was centered on a stretch of the perimeter where the wall had been replaced with a chain-link fence, topped with barbed wire. It led to a small parking lot with a handful of cars in it, and a small, utilitarian-looking building.

The second had a mailbox and an intercom next to it. An ornate 'A' above the mailbox made it clear this was a residence. Sasha pulled the car in and hit the intercom button, then leaned back to let Amanda speak.

A female voice spoke from it "Hello?"

"Hi," Amanda said. "My name's Amanda, I'm a friend of Ming's and I need to speak to him."

"Why didn't you call?"

Amanda blinked, thinking fast. "My phone is turned off."

The voice sighed and was quiet for a while. When it came back, it sounded resigned. "You fucking him?"

"What?" Amanda asked, "No, I'm just a friend. I just need to speak to him for a few minutes, and then I'll leave, I promise."

Another sign, distorted by the tiny speaker and the voice relented. "Fine, come on. Turn right at the fork, my step-dad's security is liable to shoot you if you don't."

The gate in front of them swung open on well-oiled hinges and Sasha pulled forward. For once, she was moving at a sedate pace. They came to a fork and Amanda said, "Right, here."

Sasha smirked at her. "I have ears, you know."

"I know. I'm just worried."

"Don't be worried, babe! We're making progress."

Amanda grinned. "I like when you call me babe."

"Ooh, baby..." Sasha muttered as they approached a small home, extremely modest by local standards.

They got out and walked towards the door, but before they got there, it opened and a young man stepped out. He was covered in tattoos from neck to ankle, and he wore nothing but a pair of gym shorts.

An effort to better display them, Amanda supposed. He was thin and muscular, and had even more piercings than Amanda did. His hair was cropped close, with sharp, tribal designs cut into it. Beneath his ink, his skin was pale and dotted with freckles, and the bright green color of his hair was contrasted by the rusty orange color of his eyebrows.

He walked with the same exaggerated bravado Mike had walked with in the security footage. But when he saw the two women, he stopped. His body language shifted, becoming uncertain.

"Yo, ladies," he said, his voice, at least, was steady and cocky. "What's up?"

Amanda didn't beat around the bush. "Do you know where Mike is?"

Ming pointed to a group of chairs, a question on his face. Amanda didn't get it. Was he asking permission to sit down? She shrugged and walked over, taking a seat. Sasha and Ming joined her, Ming still carrying himself almost like he was expecting a blow at any time.

"Naw, I ain't seen Mike in a while. Been looking for him, myself. Last time I saw him, he was with you," he nodded to Amanda.

"Where was that?"

"Seriously?" Ming asked.

Amanda nodded, "Listen, Ming. I need to find Mike. I don't know where he is, so I'm tracking down every lead I can right now. I just need to know as much as you can tell me about Mike, so that I know where to look next. So all I need is for you to pretend like I don't know anything, and answer all my questions, okay?" As soon as she'd spoken, she wondered where that pushiness had come from. She decided it must have been an instinctive reaction to his body language. He appeared weak, so she was projecting strength.

Ming looked scared. He nodded and swallowed hard. "Yeah, yeah, I get it. Sure. Uh, we were at Mike's place, and he was trying to act all high class and shit. You guys were dressed up nice, the way you do, and were having a dinner party. Made me dress up nice and shit, too. We had dinner, then we sat around drinking and smoking for a while, and that was it."

"You said we were dressed up nice 'the way I do'. What does that mean?"

"What? Why are you asking-"

Amanda glowered at him and he cut himself off. "Right, no problem. You guys came from different backgrounds. You know, high class girl, low class guy. Some real Romeo and Juliet shit. So you guys used to alternate your date nights. One night, you'd dress like a street walker and you and Mike would go gambling and drinking with the Blue Tiger Crew. The next one, Mike would put on a suit and you'd go to the opera or some shit."

Amanda glanced at Sasha, her eyes shining. Sasha grinned back. The prospect of getting actual answers from someone who actually knew was exciting.

"How did Mike and I meet?"

"You guys met at Viridian. I think you hired him, yourself. He was so damn proud of that job, man.

Mike could bang like nobody's business. Had a body count by the time he was sixteen. All full of bluster and attitude, but the man could fight, he could work people, and he could keep track of his hustles, you know? But he never really wanted to be a banger. When he got that job, the first thing he did was get beat out of the Blue Tigers.

"Spencer, the boss, he didn't like it, but he'd made the rules himself. They whooped Mike's ass, to remind him of what happens to snitches, he swore on his mother's grave never to talk to the cops, and that was that.

"Mike wanted to go straight. He used to talk about joining the Army, before he got pinched the first time and couldn't enlist any more. When you guys started picking up street kids to help them work security, it was the best thing that ever happened to him.

"And then you two started seeing each other at some point. I don't know all the details. I know he thought you were this aloof, unapproachable bitch, until one day… You guys were just an item. That's all I really know."

Amanda nodded. "So I was part of the group that went out to find street kids."

"Naw," Ming shook his head and gestured vaguely in Amanda's direction. "Y'all were security. Like field operatives, or some shit. The badasses."

Huh. Well, that explained the idiosyncrasies about her body, she supposed. It kind of ruled out her being Rachel, with Rachel working for their robotics department.

She caught Sasha eyeing her with a funny expression, but she put it out of her head. Was that apprehension? Probably sympathy, or rather, sympathy as filtered through her social anxiety.

"Do you have any idea where I could find Mike? Anywhere he could have gone after a... A traumatic experience?"

Ming leaned forward, his curiosity piqued. "Holy shit, were you guys involved in that shootout? I tried to find out, but I got shut down hard when I called…"

Amanda thought quickly. She needed an appropriate response. She decided to run with her instincts. "I'm not at liberty to talk about that," she snapped, "Just answer the question, please."

Ming nodded, leaning back quickly, trying to make himself look small and unthreatening.

"Yeah, no problem. I'm just worried about my bro, you know? I honestly don't know. He's not allowed to go to the Blue Tigers hangout. He might have crashed with one of the guys from the Crew, but I didn't know them real well, so I don't know which one."

"Do you know where Mike lives?"

"Yeah, he got an apartment when he got that job. I got the address right here." He showed Amanda his empty palm, then slowly reached behind his back to produce a phone. Amanda tried not to imagine where he'd been keeping it.

"What's your phone's name?"

"Amanda's phone," she answered. An address appeared in her field of view.

"Thank you," she said, forcing her voice to remain level.

"Yeah, no problem. Is, uh… Is this an official thing?" he asked, rubbing his fingers together.

Amanda blinked, trying to figure out what he meant. She glanced at Sasha, who gave her a pointed look, and then answered for her. "It's semi-official. Best we can do is, uh, Amanda, how much petty cash you got?"

Ahh, Amanda figured it out. "Two hundred," she said.

Ming looked disappointed, but nodded. Amanda thought about moncy to her BCI and it flashed up the balance in her digital wallet. She took a split second to marvel at the jeweler's generosity, and then thought about transferring it. A list of nearby devices popped up. She found "Ming" in the list and transferred it two hundred, then sent two thousand to Sasha's phone while she was at it.

Sasha's phone dinged, and she pulled it out of her purse as the two women stood.

"Thank you, Ming," Amanda said as Sasha gaped at her phone. "You've been very helpful."

"No problem. Hey, if you guys ever start hiring more bangers, keep me in mind. I got a count, too," he pointed at a pair of crosses tattooed on his shoulder. "I hung with Mike as long as I knew him. Maybe he coulda taken me in a scrap, but I'd have made him hurt for it, you know? And I know people, I've ran as many hustles as he did. Whatever Mike did for you guys, I can, too. I promise."

Amanda nodded, "I'll keep that in mind. Thank you again." She beckoned to Sasha and headed for the car.

Before she'd gone two steps, a pair of large men in body armor, cradling assault rifles stepped from behind a tall hedge. "What's your business, here?" the first one demanded of Amanda.

"None of yours," she shot back, taking another step towards the vehicle. The man stepped sideways, interposing himself between her and the car.

"I'm responsible for security on the Hopper estate, and there are two people I don't recognize, on property. It is absolutely my business."

Sasha stepped up next to Amanda and scowled at the guard. Amanda did a double take at the image she presented. This wasn't the same scowl Sasha wore when she was thinking, or embarrassed. This was a hard, cold look that radiated danger. In the face of this scowl, Amanda became hyper aware of the width of Sasha's shoulders, the thickness of her arms and the way she was standing, legs shoulder-width apart, both hands clutching her purse in front of her chest, where she could drop it and move in an instant.

Amanda caught on and primed herself to send 'flytrap' to her BCI.

"You like butt stuff?" Sasha asked the guard, who blinked at her in surprise at the out-of-the-blue question. "What?" He asked in response.

"I asked if you like butt stuff. Because it's better for you if you do, seeing as how you're about to spend the next half hour pulling that rifle out of your ass."

The guard chuckled, but there were nervous undertones to the laugh. He looked to his partner, who seemed a lot more relaxed, having not been subjected to Sasha's cold look. Amanda filled the gap, glaring at the man, ready to change states and go on the offensive the instant he moved.

The first guard looked at Amanda again, and said, "Well? Am I gonna have to have you arrested?"

"We were just leaving," Amanda snapped, "And I swear to all that's holy, if you stop us from leaving I will not rest until I've broken every goddamn bone in your pathetic, out-of-shape bully body."

The second guard shouldered his rifle while the first gaped at Amanda.

"Hey you fuckheads! They're with me!" Ming's voice sounded from behind them.

Both guards turned to look at him.

"The fuck is wrong with you dipshits?! You see where they're parked, you know the fucking rules. Suzie and I can have over anyone we want, as long as they stay on our corner. I'm calling Brent right fucking now, I'm so sick of you two assholes fucking around out here." Ming stepped up next to the two women, his phone held up to his ear.

"Fine, whatever," the first guard said with false nonchalance. "You know, we keep you two safe, too."

"I keep myself safe, bitch. You just get in the fucking way. Brent? Hey man, it's Ming. Yeah... You got it. They're right here, harassing my guests. Yeah, no problem."

Ming stepped forward and handed the first guard his phone. The guard kept his eyes from meeting anyone else's as he brought the phone up. Amanda heard yelling over the line and took the opportunity to step around the man, into the car. Sasha got in the driver's side and started the engine.

"You think we should stick around to see them eat shit?" Sasha asked, shooting Amanda a mischievous grin.

"No, let's just go. I'm just glad we didn't have to fight them."

"I dunno," Sasha said, "You were gonna break every bone in his out of shape, bully body, remember?" Amanda snorted a laugh. "He was making me angry," she explained. "But you? With the butt stuff comment?"

Sasha laughed "I heard it in a movie once. I've always wanted to use it. What did you think? Did I sound cool?"

"Sasha, you scared the shit out of me when you walked up like that. I thought for sure you were about to stomp both of them into the dirt before I could even react."

They both laughed.

They drove around the circular driveway and returned to the gate, which opened automatically for them. They pulled out onto the street and began heading back towards downtown.

"I don't think we should go to Mike's apartment, first." Sasha said.

"What? Why?"

"Well, I mean, if he was there, Ming would know. He said he's been looking for him, too. I think we should look for the other guy. What did you say his name was? Christopher?"

"cristobol," Amanda said, "But I have no idea where he is. I don't know who he works for or anything about him really. I just feel like I was supposed to find him."

"Right, but he's neck-deep in whatever the fuck is going on, right? And he came by the other jewelry shop to ask Miss Chan questions. That means he's some kind of an agent, or an investigator."

"I don't see why that- Wait, you think he'll stake out Chan Jewels?"

Sasha nodded and grinned.

"Okay," Amanda said, "I mean, I guess that's not a bad plan, at all. You're good at this."

Sasha squealed and turned on the radio to a fast-paced rock song. They rocketed away at her usual speed and Amanda couldn't help but laugh at her excitement.

Accused

Tuesday, December 29th, 2759

They parked across the street and half a block down from the police perimeter holos in front of the store. Amanda managed to get a clearish image of Chris/David's face from her BCI and share it with Sasha. They took turns walking around the block every half hour, checking the parked cars and the tables of curbside diners for him.

After four hours, Amanda got out to walk the block while Sasha left to get some food. She returned after Amanda had made one and a half circuits and parked in a different spot, on the opposite side of the street. When Amanda climbed back in, Sasha showed off her purchases.

"I got food, of course, but I bet you have to pee, right?"

Amanda nodded, "Yeah, I was going to go down the alley and squat before we ate." Sasha shook her head, "No need, look." She opened a plastic bag and removed a bottle with an oddly-shaped cup on the mouth. The cup looked like a cheap jock-strap, but lacked any air holes. "You just, ah…" Sasha placed the mouth of the cup against her crotch, squeezed the bottle and then slowly let it expand again. "The suction helps prevent any leakage."

Amanda accepted the bottle from Sasha, who pulled another one out of the bag. "Where in the world did you find these?" she asked as she looked around to make sure no-one was watching. She unbuttoned her jeans, which immediately relaxed and expanded, then tugged them down and carefully used the cup. The relief was palpable, a pressure off her bladder, a weight she hadn't really comprehended until it was gone.

"My god, that feels good." She set the bottle in the center console while she pulled her pants and panties back up.

"There's a literal spy shop next to the dim sum place. I used that money you sent me, which you didn't have to do, by the way, to buy some gear. Let me get the food out and we can look at it while we eat."

They ate shrimp dumplings and spring rolls while they examined the haul. Sasha had a directional microphone, a pair of handheld tasers, binoculars and tiny, collapsible periscopes. She'd already discarded all the packaging and installed batteries, and they came out of the plastic bags from the dim sum shop ready to go.

"The microphone looks very handy," Amanda noted around a mouthful of spring roll.

Sasha beamed at her and got the thing set up and aimed at the jewelry shop. She listened through a pair of headphones for a moment, then offered the headphones to Amanda. Amanda placed them on her head and heard the echoes and reverberation of the street sounds off the remains of the storefront.

There was nothing interesting about the sound, but Amanda left the headphones on, anyways.

They finished their food, Sasha used her own piss bottle and they agreed that the bottles were the coolest thing Sasha had gotten. Or at least the most useful.

That's when Amanda heard a voice.

"Gotta be something…"

The voice faded as Amanda jerked forward. She quickly pointed the mic back at the storefront, but still heard nothing. She panned it around, up and down, left and right until she heard a little crunch. It was when she had it aimed at the broken window. She used the little viewfinder on the mic to aim it at the window again.

"I can't find anything," the voice said. "Yeah, she was here. She came out of the back. Gods, Cindy, she knew my damn name for crying out loud."

Gods? That was an odd expletive. She wondered who would use it.

The dominant religion in the United Empire of Earth is Norse Paganism. Norse Paganism is a polytheistic religion focusing on-

Amanda silenced it with a thought. Draughtgen again? Interesting… Amanda listened some more.

"I don't know," the voice said, and Amanda carefully listened, comparing it to her memories of Chris/David's voice. "She acted like she didn't know what the hell was going on. I believe you! I don't know who else she could be, either. Fine, hold on, let me look. Uh… Yeah, that's definitely her. She had black hair with maroon stripes in it, though. Same face, though. Yeah. Well, I'll let you know if I find her, I…

How many times do I have to say that I don't know? Gods, she fell out of the car while I was doing seventy. The hospitals don't know anything, but I doubt she'd need a hospital, in any event. Yeah. No, I think they got her. Maybe. I mean, we could try another angle. Yeah, yeah, yeah. I know, I'm just reluctant to let it go. This was our chance to do something good, babe. Much better than on New Canada. Alright, I'm…"

Amanda had heard enough. She was sure it was him.

"He's inside the shop right now! I need to move, I think he's about to leave."

"Go, go!" Sasha encouraged her, grabbing the food packaging and mic from Amanda's lap. Amanda jumped out of the car, looked around to make sure no-one was paying attention to her, then darted down an alley to approach the shop from behind. She turned the corner onto the larger alley behind the shop and stopped when she saw a patrol bot there.

It stood stock still in the center of the alley, facing her. It didn't react to her sudden appearance. Amanda took a tentative step forward, and the bot didn't move. She eyed it for a moment before noticing something sticking out of its neck.

Patrol bots were all over the city, and she had seen dozens of them. None of them had that thing sticking out of her neck. Amanda took several more steps forward and the bot still didn't react. Growing bolder, she walked right up to it and eyed the protuberance.

It was made of a different metal. Some kind of runic writing was printed on it, different from the Hanzi or English one could find all over New Kowloon. The bot was clearly disabled. The device protruding from its neck was almost certainly responsible.

She walked carefully around it and approached the holo that marked the back of Chan Jewels. At that moment, Chris/David stepped through it and froze when he saw her.

"You're Amanda, right?"

Amanda nodded. "And you're David."

"Gods," he muttered, "Please, for the love of all that's holy, call me Chris or Cristobol."

"Okay Cristobol," she said, carefully enunciating the name. "Can you answer some questions for me?"

"Not here," he said, looking around.

"Do you have someplace we can talk?" Amanda asked him. He nodded. "Come with me."

Sasha gave a little yelp of fright from behind her. David started, a small handgun appearing in his left hand in the blink of an eye.

"Stop! She's with me," Amanda said quickly. She called back over her shoulder, "It's okay, Sasha, come on."

"That's Sasha, huh?" Amanda gave him a look. He really did have some odd mannerisms.

"Yes," she said, "and she's with me. I trust her." Sasha came up and stood next to Amanda. "This is him?" she asked.

"Yeah. This is Chris-slash-David," she said, deliberately using the name he didn't like. She didn't appreciate him pulling a gun on her only friend.

Chris/David groaned and wiped his face with one hand. "Gods… Whatever. Come on, both of you. My car's over here." he nodded in the opposite direction from which they'd come.

"Come on," Amanda told Sasha, "We can trust him." Sasha didn't look so sure, but this had been her idea, so she went along with it.

He pulled the device from the patrol bot's neck, and they followed him down the alley, and then through the gap between two buildings to the road, where the same white car he'd driven the previous night was parked. He pointed at it and all four doors opened.

They climbed in and took off. Chris/David drove the same way Sasha did; with reckless abandon. They swerved in and out of traffic, peeling tires around turns and roaring the engine on clear stretches.

"Do you have to drive like that?" Amanda asked. She could ignore it coming from someone as helpful as Sasha had been, but memories of flying out of the same seat she currently occupied the previous night was making it harder to accept now.

"Fuck yes, I do. If anyone's following us, they're gonna stick out like a sore thumb," he responded. Amanda signed and willed her butthole to unpucker.

It didn't work. At least it might provide some suction to stick her to the seat, she thought.

"I hope they're not using a fucking flier," Chris/David muttered, checking the mirrors and then leaning forward and looking up.

They drove for a while. Chris/David took them out of the city and onto a highway. He eventually slowed down to a mere thirty kilometers over the speed limit, and they kept that up for most of an hour.

As the sun was setting, he took an exit onto a tiny, two-lane road, and they spent another half an hour driving down that, until it turned into a dirt road. Several kilometers later, he turned off into the forest, down several hundred meters of what looked like an ancient driveway, to a small, run-down shack.

"Okay, we're safe here. We can talk, rest and plan the next step."

He got out and led them inside. Amanda gaped as she entered the building.

On the outside, it looked like any other run-down shack in the woods. The kind of place you'd expect to be abandoned, full of dusty furniture dating back to the original colony days. But inside, the walls and floors were in perfect repair, clean and simple. The place had a utilitarian quality to it, with little furniture and a lot of equipment. Crates with a military feel to them were stacked against the wall. A desk stood in one corner, expensive computer equipment sitting on top of it. A pair of cots stood against another wall, and Amanda could see four more cots folded up and stacked in the corner.

"This is a safehouse?" she asked.

"Yeah, sort of. This is a secured site. Don't mess with anything; everything's got DNA readers in it, and it *will* set off a shit-ton of thermal charges if it doesn't recognize you."

Amanda stuck her hands in her pockets and looked at Sasha, who balked a little and did the same.

"Okay, so you want to ask me some questions, right? Well, I have one question for you. If you answer my question, I'll answer yours, sound fair?" Chris/David grabbed a folding chair and opened it up, then sat it on the floor. He repeated this twice more, then sat on the last one.

"I think I can work with that." Amanda wasn't sure if she really could, but she was prepared to at least try. She didn't know who this guy was working for, but she'd had the sense for as long as she could remember that she needed to find him. That didn't sound like something she'd feel if he was a threat.

"Alright. So the only thing I need to know is where you put the drive. If you have it on you, that's golden. If not, just tell me where it is."

"What drive?" Amanda asked. "I don't know anything about a drive."

"What? Listen, don't play games, you already know that I know, and I know that you know."

"I really don't know. You don't understand. The first thing I remember is waking up in an alley, the night before last, naked and covered in blood and injured. I don't remember who I am, or how I got there. I'm trying to find out what happened to me."

Chris/David leaned back in his chair. "Shit, are you for real?"

"She is for real," Sasha said, surprising Amanda. She'd remained quiet through the last two interviews. Amanda wondered why she'd spoken up now.

"I am. I'm not joking. I've almost died several times now. Listen, I just want to find Mike, to find out who I am, and try to get back to my life."

Chris/David shook his head slowly in disbelief. "I can't… I gotta call this in. Hold on." He pulled out his phone and placed it against his ear.

"Yeah, it's me. Listen, I've got her. She's right here with me, and she brought some goth chick along with her, Sasha. I don't know, probably. I mean, who else would it be? Here's the thing, though. She's telling me that she can't remember anything before waking up naked in an alley night before last. Yup. Yeah. Thor's taint, I don't fucking know. I mean, I guess. I don't see why not. We can… Yeah, that's what I'm thinking. Okay. I'll ask her, then I'll go. I'll look, and if I find it, I'll come back. You can send the retrieval team. No, Site, uh…" he stood and walked to the desk, tapping on the computer interface there. "Seventeen. Yup. Okay. Alright, let me ask her. I'll call when I'm on the way. Gotcha, out."

He hung up the phone and sat back down. "Okay, here's the deal. I need that drive. I believe you, that you don't know where it is. But I absolutely need it, or my whole job is fucked. So, tell me where, exactly, you woke up, and I *think* I can retrace your steps and find where you hid it."

"So what's on this drive?" Amanda asked. Chris/David shook his head.

"Nuh huh, my question was where the drive is. When I have that drive, I'll come back here and let you pick my brain for anything germane to your situation. Until then, you haven't done your part yet. So tell me where, *exactly* you woke up, and when, and then I'm gonna go try and find the drive. When I get back, if I found it, I'll give you hours to chat me up, okay?"

Amanda stood. She didn't like this. She was beginning to wonder how wise it was to trust this man. She looked at Sasha, who gave her an expectant look and tilted her head towards Chris/David.

Amanda sighed. She was out of her depth, and didn't know what to do. Both of the others seemed to think she should tell him, so… Fuck it.

"Do you have a map?"

Chris/David promised to be back before the next night. He went around and fiddled with some of the equipment, then had each of them press their thumbs on a scanner. They looked like thumbprint scanners, but Chris/David said they were DNA scanners. Amanda didn't know how they'd get a DNA sample without actually taking a sample, but she supposed it didn't matter.

They could use the gear he'd authorized them on. It was security equipment; cameras and motion sensors scattered around the shack. Once he'd shown them how to use it, he opened a crate and pulled out two military rifles. He handed them over, gave them a rundown of how to use them, then stacked some magazines on the desk for them.

"If anyone shows up, you kill the shit out of them, then go touch that thing, right there," he pointed to the computer on the desk, "And then you get the hell out of here as quick as you can. You've got fifteen seconds from the time you touched it until the thermal charges go off, and trust me, you don't want to be inside when they do. There's a river, about half a kilometer straight out the back door and a boat under a camo net next to it. Take the boat, and get the fuck out of this whole country. You won't be safe unless you can make it to the Confederate border, understand?"

Amanda told him she understood and Sasha chimed in her agreement. Chris/David, finally satisfied that they could survive the night without him, left.

Amanda watched the taillights shrink until they turned onto the dirt road and vanished. She turned back to the house to find Sasha standing there.

Her face was twisted in pain. Tears stained her cheeks as she stared at Amanda.

"Sasha, what's wrong?!" Amanda rushed forward, shocked concern creeping up her spine and twisting her gut.

"You lied," Sasha said.

"What? What did I lie about?"

"You lied about everything!" Sasha shrieked with sudden intensity. She swung a fist that caught Amanda on the side of the head and knocked her to the ground.

"Sasha! What are you doing?" Amanda scrambled backwards as Sasha stalked forward, fists clenched at her side.

"You went behind my back, Amanda! You were going to just leave me there!"

"I don't know what you're talking about!"

Sasha took a final step forward and then kicked Amanda in the side. Pain exploded through her torso and she cried out as she was bowled over.

The word popped into her head. Flytrap. She almost sent it to her BCI, but then she remembered what she'd done to the men who had captured her. No, she didn't want to kill Sasha.

Sasha, apparently, didn't feel the same. She reached behind her back and produced Amanda's stolen handgun. Amanda's eyes went wide.

"I trusted you," Sasha sobbed. "And you trusted me, until you didn't." She raised the gun and fired. Amanda felt a hot poker stab through her leg.

"Sasha, what are you doing? I don't know what's going on! Please, just put the gun down and tell me what's wrong!" Panic and fear turned on each other and fought for supremacy. Panic won, and Amanda scrambled backwards as fast as she could, the bullet in her leg sending a shock of agony through her with every motion.

Sasha adjusted her aim up, and Amanda ran out of options.

Flytrap

The pain in her leg didn't actually get any better, but her tolerance for pain skyrocketed. She rolled quickly to the side right as Sasha squeezed the trigger again. She came smoothly to her feet and charged Sasha from the side, leaping at the last second to throw a shoulder into Sasha's side and grab the wrist of her gun hand.

They tumbled to the ground, Amanda slammed her hand down hard and Sasha lost her grip on the gun. Fists flew, faster than Amanda could keep track of, but she was moving on instinct, anyways. She didn't need to track the exact count of blows.

She managed to grab Sasha's wrist again and got both hands on it. She leaned back, drawing out Sasha's arm across her body and got her legs around her neck and torso. She arched her back and felt the elbow crackle and then snap. Sasha growled and twisted, pulling against her own broken elbow to twist her body and bring her other fist down on Amanda's nose.

Pain exploded in her face and she felt hot blood spurt out across her lips. Sasha twisted again and pulled her arm free. She rolled away and came to her feet, already rushing back in. Amanda rolled towards her, instead of away, taking her by surprise and tripping her. Sasha stumbled, but didn't lose her feet.

Amanda came up behind her and got her arms around Sasha's waist. She didn't use a complicated martial arts technique, but rather, bodily lifted the other woman up, over her head and fell backwards.

Sasha's weight slammed into her, driving the air from her lungs, but Amanda heard her head crack against the hard-packed dirt. A part of her mind felt a surge of satisfaction at the sound, while another part screamed in horror. She pushed Sasha off of her, got upright and looked down. A trickle of blood ran from the back of her skull and Amanda froze for a second.

In that instant, she heard it. The alarm, coming from the shack. She had no idea how much of the fight it had been ringing through. She turned to it and took a running step back, but a hand clamped down on her ankle and she flipped forward into the dirt. She got her hands up just in time.

She rolled as soon as she hit, cocking a leg and lashing out. She caught Sasha in the hips and threw her legs out backwards. Sasha flopped down next to her and Amanda swung a fist around at the back of her skull.

It was the perfect blow. The muscle of her hand would cushion it just enough to prevent a crack in Sasha's skull, but nonetheless strike with the force to concuss her. Still dangerous, of course, but much safer for Sasha than almost any other finishing strike Amanda knew in her flytrap state.

Both parts of her mind approved of it. It was the best possible outcome. Of course, it never landed.

Her clenched fist was mere centimeters from Sasha's skull when the beam from the taser locked up every muscle in her body and made her vision flash black rapidly. Right next to her, another taser beam shone on Sasha and she suddenly tensed up, her eyelids fluttering rapidly.

"Blue Top, this is Blue-3, I've got both targets here, incap on the ground."

Multiple flashlight beams shined on them, circling around. Amanda's vision continued to flash to black and back, but more slowly now that the taser was off. She was still wracked with weakness and couldn't move.

A loud whoosh sounded and a wave of intense heat washed over her. She heard several voices cry out in alarm as a golden light suffused the driveway. Someone must have touched something inside.

A face she didn't recognize appeared above her. "Yeah," it said, "This is them. Good job, Blue-3." He raised a device and pointed it at Amanda, and everything went black.

Apprehended

Wednesday, December 30th, 2759

Amanda regained consciousness strapped to a chair.

This time, the room was clean. Four white walls, with a small white light at the top center of each one. The ceiling was painted sky blue, the floor painted a rich brown. She was naked again, wrists, ankles and waist clamped to the chair by thick metal bands. The chair was bolted to the floor. There was a clean, square bandage on her leg where she'd been shot.

She barely had time to adjust to her new circumstances when the door opened and two men in neat suits walked in. One was tall and thin, with handsome features that Amanda instinctively wanted to punch. The other had darker skin, and was shorter and stockier. He looked like an accountant with his bushy mustache, Amanda thought.

"Good of you to join us, Amanda. I'm Bob, and this is my associate, Clarence. We'd like to ask you some questions, after which we can discuss what we can do for you, alright?"

Bob retrieved a chair from behind her, and Clarence did the same. They dragged them around to face her and sat down. Clarence's eyes swept up and down her body several times, and a flash of disgust passed through her.

Bob didn't wait for Amanda to answer. "So tell us what you did with the drive, first."

"I don't know," Amanda mumbled.

"You don't know? How do you not know?"

"I don't know anything. I don't remember anything. I didn't do anything. I don't want anything but to find Mike, and to find out who I was. I can't fucking help you."

"Oh, come on. Don't be difficult. We're not unreasonable here. All you have to do…" Bob leaned forward, his eyes locked onto Amandas, a friendly smile on his face. "…is talk to me."

"I am talking, asshole. I don't remember anything before I woke up naked the other night in an alley. I don't know where your precious drive is. I don't even know *what* it is. I just don't fucking know."

Bob leaned back, a frown marring his features. "Amanda, I don't understand. You had a *place* here. You were one of us. You had authority and agency and freedom… You had money. A personal expense account with no limit, for christ's sake. Anything you wanted. You can still have that, you know. I mean, of course, there's going to be some disciplinary action, but we're not in the habit of throwing away valuable resources. All you have to do is talk to me."

"I don't want any of that," Amanda said. "I don't care. I just want to know who I am. I want to find Mike."

"Mike Flannigan?" Clarence asked. Amanda looked up. "Yes, yes. Mike Flannigan. I just want to find him. I'd give you the drive if I had it."

Bob and Clarence exchanged a glance. Bob looked upset. After a second, he turned back to Amanda, his eyes full of sympathy.

"I'm afraid I have some bad news, Amanda. Mike is dead."

"What?" That wasn't right. It couldn't be. She'd been searching for him for too long for him to be dead.

"No, he can't be dead! I have to find him!"

"Amanda, listen to me," Bob said, but she shook her head furiously. "No! He's not dead! Tell me where he is!"

"Amanda-" Bob cut himself off and stood. "I'll be right back," he said, and walked out.

Amanda glared at Clarence for several minutes. Neither of them spoke.

Bob walked back in, a tablet in his hands. He turned it towards Amanda as he sat down.

"Amanda, watch. We just got a hold of this footage last night. It's… Well, you'll see."

Amanda looked at the tablet. It was obviously security footage. The flat 3D display showed an apartment cluttered with electronics. Nothing happened for several minutes except for a few dust motes floating across the screen.

Suddenly, she heard pounding footsteps coming from the tablet speakers. Several pairs of feet, moving close together, stomping on a wooden floor. Two people burst into view, carrying a third. Amanda leaned forward to see better. The figure being carried was her. She was dressed in black, tactical gear, and blood was pouring from her head, splattering the floor. She didn't recognize one of the men carrying her, but the other was Mike. He was dressed similarly to her, and he had a rifle slung across his back.

As she watched, the two men carried her to a kitchen table, sweeping off a bunch of small devices and trash. They threw her on it, and Mike started talking.

"Alright, now do your thing, Nash." He sounded panicked.

"Jesus, Mike... Give me a second, I need tools. Do you know how to open her up?"

"Yes, get your shit. Hurry, man!"

Nash ran out of view, while Mike undid her armored vest. He got it off and flung it to the side, unbuttoning her shirt, next. He ripped it off, and got the rest of her clothes off before Nash returned. "I need a taser," Mike said.

Nash set his stuff down on the table next to Amanda and handed something to Mike. Mike took it and fiddled with it, spreading out two tongs that protruded from the front by bending them. He placed the device against Amanda's chest and triggered it.

Amanda looked down at her own chest. The marks were gone now, but she imagined she could see a little discoloration where they had been. She looked back at the tablet.

Her head had distorted oddly, opening up in the back like a clamshell. It was different from what she'd seen the man in the video at Sasha's do. This was more structured. More deliberate. As if she'd been built to be repaired, and the Seven series was not. The blood flowing out of her tapered off as her head opened completely.

Mike grabbed her and flipped her over onto her back, gently, cradling her misshapen head in his arms. "Here you go," he said, and Nash stepped forward.

"Do you have the parts you told me about?"

"Yeah," Mike dug into the messenger bag at his side, "Right here." He pulled out several pieces of electronics and set them down. Nash poured over them, "Okay, this one, right here should work. Let me see."

He dug around in Amanda's open skull for several minutes. He grabbed tools; magnetic screwdrivers and pliers and little picks. After a while, he drew out a part that had a bullet hole through it and dropped it on the table. He grabbed the part he'd selected and carefully placed it into her head.

"Man, these parts were *not* meant to go together. She's gonna lose a *lot* of her memory, man."

"I don't fucking care, Nash, just fucking save her!"

Mike's voice was different. The brash cockiness she'd heard in the jewelry store footage was gone, replaced by an urgent, commanding tone. It was the voice of a man pushed to the limit, and struggling with all he had to push back.

"Alright, dude, hold on."

Nash continued to work for several more minutes.

"Alright man, I think that's it. Close her back up. She should finish charging her capacitors in maybe ten, fifteen minutes, then she'll boot up."

"She's coming back?" Mike asked.

"Yeah, I promise, man. I tapped the maintenance port, everything's fine. Well, working, anyway. Listen, she's gonna lose a *lot* of her memories. I mean a lot. She... She might not remember you, dude."

Mike shook his head slowly. "It doesn't matter, Nash. As long as she's alive. That's all I need. If she doesn't remember me, then I'll introduce myself again. We'll meet again, have our first kiss again... As long as she's safe."

"She's not safe, man! You guys have pissed off fucking Viridian, for fuck's sake! They're not gonna stop coming after you until they get you, now."

Mike shook his head. "We'll stop them. We'll run. Whatever it takes."

Nash stumbled without warning, collapsing against the table. He looked down at his side, where a bloodstain was rapidly spreading on his shirt. "What the fuck?" he gasped, before his head abruptly jerked to the side and sprayed blood.

Mike spun, jamming the taser down on the studs on her lower back. He triggered it and her head closed back up. He grabbed her, hunching over her body as his armored vest jerked and he grunted in pain. He scooped her up in his arms and ran out of view.

The footage shifted perspective. A different camera. She could see part of the table in the lower left corner of the screen, one of Nash's hands just barely in view. Mike ran to a window and quickly shoved it open with one foot. He peered out, looking down and then to the right.

"Please, remember where you left the thing, babe. When you wake up, just grab it and go." He looked down at her, and she saw a tear drip down onto her chest. "I love you, Amanda," he said, and then he tossed her out the window, leaning far out himself as she went.

He quickly pulled it shut and unslung the rifle off of his shoulder. He knelt down in a firing stance and aimed it back towards the entrance. The incoming gunfire had stopped, and he kneeled there, motionless for a minute. She heard a loud bang, and then Mike started firing.

"Come on, you motherfuckers!" he yelled as he pumped round after round at the door.

The wall behind him began to splinter as whoever he was shooting at began returning fire. Mike kept shooting until the lever of his rifle locked back, and then he expertly reloaded. He slapped the lever forward right as his left sleeve puffed out with a spray of blood. Mike didn't react. He raised the rifle back up to his shoulder and began shooting again.

Amanda gasped. She felt tears welling up in her eyes.

Another bullet struck him in the neck. Blood began to pour from the wound, but he still didn't react. He fired until he ran dry, and then reloaded again.

She gasped again.

A third bullet struck him, just above the armor on his right side. He grunted, but kept shooting.

Amanda sobbed. The tears ran down her cheeks and dripped off her chin.

A fourth and fifth bullet hit him, at almost the same time.

She cried out, willing something to change, someone to appear to save him. But nothing did. No one came.

Mike managed to reload again, but then his hand slipped when he tried to push the lever forward. Another bullet struck his leg, knocking it out from under him. He grunted again, got the lever slapped forward and fired twice more down the hall.

Another bullet struck his neck. Right in the center. He dropped the rifle and his legs stopped kicking.

Amanda's breathing hitched and she wept openly as she watched him. His own breathing was labored. She could hear him wheezing around the holes in his neck as he struggled for each lungful of air. Shadows appeared at the bottom of the view. She couldn't see who cast them.

A gunshot rang out and Mike's head snapped back. She saw the back half of his skull simply disintegrate and she cried out at the tablet in protest. The recording cut off, and all she could see was her own tortured face, reflected back at her.

"I'm starting to believe you," Bob said.

Amanda stared at him, shocked. "Believe what?" she demanded.

"That you don't remember anything. Your reaction… If I didn't know better, I'd swear you actually cared about him."

"What the fuck is wrong with you?!" Amanda screamed. "What the fuck did you expect me to do, laugh?! What the fuck?!"

Bob jerked back at her outburst. He tapped the tablet a few times and then held it up again. "I expected something more… Collected," he said. The screen lit up with another 3D recording. This one showed her. She was dressed in business pants and a white tank top, pacing through a well-lit garden at night.

"Yeah," the recorded version of her said. "I honeypotted one of the street kids we picked up. Mike. Yeah, Mike Flannigan. I know. He *is* cute, that's why I picked him. Anyways, he's got his finger on this town's pulse. Just got out of the biggest gang in Tai Po, has friends in Manyan, Central, Oldtown and Downtown. He's got a built-in excuse to get me out of the building and out around town. Yeah. No, he's a sweet kid under all that bravado. The loyal type. Even if he suspects, I'm like 99% convinced I can read him in. No, of course not. Not unless I have to. The fewer people who know, the better."

The recording cut back off.

Bob was talking, "...blue team, that wasn't us here on White team. We don't kick down doors and shoot first like that. I'm sorry, Amanda, we really didn't know how much he meant to you. I wouldn't have shown you this if I'd known. I'd like you to know that…"

Amanda tuned him out and continued to stare at her reflection in shock. How could she do that? Mike had died protecting her. He'd told her he loved her and then turned back and stood against their pursuers, laying down his own life to protect her.

And she'd put him up to it. Manipulated him into it. The guilt racked her body and she shook with more sobs. Sadness at the loss of Mike, anger at herself for getting him killed, frustration at being strapped to this chair, confusion about Sasha…

She collapsed into herself and sat there and cried. She didn't know for how long. When she finally began to register the world around her, Bob and Clarence were gone.

She looked around, trying to figure out… She didn't know. What to do, where she could go, how she should feel. She needed to figure out everything. And she didn't know how to figure out anything.

Her BCI chimed in; a graphic showing a view of her own lap, strapped into the chair, with a timestamp below it and a rewind symbol in the middle. She focused on it and it rewound several minutes.

"Well, hell, Bob, I think you broke her," Clarence said, underneath the sounds of Amanda sobbing.

"Seems like. Well, whatever. I tried. Just… I guess we can just hand her over to recycling. Have them pull her memory modules out, give them to the lab boys for decryption. Send the body to get a couple tissue samples for cloning and then scrap the rest. Come on, let's put the calls in now, get it moving."

"Yeah," Clarence agreed, "Might as well. I don't see her telling us anything, and the sooner we get started, the sooner the lab will have the data we need."

Shifting shadows suggested that they stood and left, but Amanda continued to sob. She cut off the recording before it could get under her skin and set her off again.

They were going to kill her. At least now, she knew what to do.

Flytrap

The confusion and pain drifted off. She examined the bands around her wrists and found that there was a button on the outside of them. A pushbutton release. Typical for private security forces, who preferred to do everything the easy way, without a whole government to insist upon a proscribed way of doing it.

She twisted her hand and stretched her fingers towards it. She couldn't quite reach it.

She twisted her hips as much as the band around her waist allowed, then made a fist and pulled it tight against the band. She tucked her shoulder in, braced and jerked hard. Her shoulder came out of the joint with a dull crack and a lightning bolt of pain from her fingertips to her neck.

She twisted her hips back, building up slack in her now limp arm. She used her chest to push her arm further into the band, then she began shaking. Her arm flopped around, the skin and muscle in her shoulder twisting painfully, but she got her hand turned out a few centimeters further. She reached her fingers back, and got the tip of her middle finger on the button. She tried to push it, but couldn't get enough force. She bore down, concentrating on willing as much power into one finger as possible. She pushed, and the button creeped in, a half millimeter, one millimeter, and then it clicked.

The band snapped open.

She pulled her arm free and used it to unlock the other bands. She stood up and grabbed the back of the chair. She twisted again, then pulled, straining. She felt her shoulder pop back into the socket, and then rotated it experimentally a few times.

A trick like that was generally a bad idea, but she'd been desperate. And it worked. She rubbed her aching shoulder and looked around the room. Other than the two chairs which the men had used, and the third which she'd been strapped to, there was nothing in it. She tried the door handle and found it unlocked. Thank god for lax private security protocols.

She stepped out into a hallway that was just as clean and spartan as the room. There were no signs on any of the doors. She picked a direction at random and walked down it until she found the end. Another door occupied the short wall. She opened it and stepped through into a large room full of equipment. Metal shelves held orderly rows of parts and tools, and another door on the far end had a green-glowing exit sign above it.

She walked through the door into another room. Two men, in security uniforms and with guns at their hips sat at a desk that held a row of holo displays. They started when she walked in.

"Hey, you're not supposed to be he-" one of them started, but Amanda was already moving. She launched a foot up at his head, curving around and putting her whole weight behind it.

The arch of her foot cracked into his head, pushing him sideways into the other guard and sending them both tumbling to the floor. Amanda stepped forward and stomped down hard on the first guard's throat. She felt it squish and crunch under her, and he immediately began squealing like a pig, pawing at his throat with both hands, desperately trying to suck in air that couldn't make it past the ruin of his windpipe.

She hauled back and soccer kicked the other guard in the face. His head snapped back, a spurt of blood erupting from his nose, and then he lay still, insensate for the moment.

She quickly dug at his waist for restraints and found them, binding the man's hands behind his back, then doing his ankles. She used his final pair of the plastic cuffs to link the two together.

The other guard was still trying to breathe, still making gurgly squealing sounds, so Amanda stomped on his neck again, and again. She felt a heavy crack on the second blow, and he went still and silent. She stripped him and pulled his clothes on herself. She finished by cinching his gun belt tightly around her waist and turned to the displays.

There were multiple scenes visible, with people in most of them. At the top left, she saw a face that caught her attention. Peering closer, she could see that it was Rachel Hornsby. She was talking animatedly to two men, who seemed to be deferring to her. Amanda touched a sound icon, and suddenly she could hear.

"...goes bad, there's going to be a price to pay, and I don't mean collectively, though it will certainly include that. You, both of you, and me are all going to find our name on arrest warrants and in the fucking news, you hear me? We need to fix this! So I don't care what you have to do, you get that fucking evidence and you make it go the fuck away. Bring it back here or destroy it in the field, I don't fucking care. Just get it. We've got the two DevSec agents already, thanks to Blue Team. That drive is the last loose end. So get out there and snip it."

Amanda looked over the others as she listened. The two men gave acknowledgements, and then the audio went silent. She got almost through the whole collection of displays when she saw something that made her freeze in place.

It was Sasha. She was strapped to a chair, naked, the same as Amanda. There were two figures with their backs to her, standing and talking to Sasha, who kept her face turned down. Amanda turned on the audio and began looking for a way to identify where the room was.

"...was going to leave me behind to deal with the fallout. So I followed her. I ducked out before White Team could lock down the building and tried to keep up, but I lost them. I kept searching and picked her up the next day by pure chance. She was walking around downtown in dirty clothes, acting strangely. I followed her for a bit, and overheard her asking about a makeup shop, which was a lucky break, because I had an informant who worked mornings in the closest makeup shop to where she was. I was gonna hide in the back, but then Amanda got there so fast, that I didn't have time. I froze, but Amanda just… She didn't recognize me. She just smiled at me and turned to the makeup. I quickly chased my contact out, and stood in for her. When Amanda got to the counter, she just… I mean, she didn't recognize me at all.

"I flirted with her. I gave her a number she could reach me at and basically hoped for the best. I figured if she didn't remember anything, she wouldn't remember her caches and safehouses and contacts. She'd need help. It worked. She called me that night, after one of the merc groups picked her up while tailing Alvares. Those idiots didn't recognize her, and tried to interrogate her about Alvares, but she got loose and killed them, then called me because she didn't have anyone else.

"I picked her up and she wanted me to take her to a hotel, but I wasn't going to let her out of my sight, at that point. I still had an apartment from my last undercover op, where I'd been posing as a med student, so I brought her there. I tried to feed her some breadcrumbs, to see if I could jog her memory.

"It didn't work, not really. She had altered her hardware somehow, I could see that from a neural imager I used on her. I don't know when or why, but it was clear that she really couldn't remember anything. So I followed her around and pushed her in the direction of finding the drive. I was going to bring it back here, use it to negotiate, get us both cut loose.

Then I was going to take her and go somewhere far away. Maybe the Empire, where we could blend in better." Sasha's voice sounded… Different. She spat out each sentence as if it was unconnected with the rest, her voice absent of any emotion.

One of the men turned to speak to the other, and Amanda recognized him as Bob, but couldn't make out what he said. He turned back to Sasha.

"When Blue Team found you, they said you two were fighting. Can you explain that?"

"I…" Sasha sighed. "I lost my shit. Being with her, all day, with her not remembering anything. It was frustrating. It took a lot out of me. When Alvares left the secure site, I knew I had the information I needed already. I snapped. I didn't intend to kill her, but then when I had the gun, I was just so… So *angry*. I wasn't thinking straight."

"Uh huh. So your plan was to trade the drive for both of your freedom, right? Have your contracts cancelled?"

"That was it, yeah."

"If you know where the drive is, we might be able to work that out. Depending on how easily we can retrieve me, maybe we could toss in some new hardware, get Amanda back up to spec. What do you say?"

"I don't know where it is. But I know where she woke up with no memories. Get me a map, I'll show you the exact spot. But Alvares is already on his way there. You'll have to move quickly."

Bob gestured to the other man, who turned and left. It wasn't Clarence. Amanda leaned back and thought for a second. The timestamps on the recording claimed it was Wednesday, at 1:12AM. That meant it had only been a few hours. Chris/David would have had just enough time to get to the spot by now. She was sure that Viridian could field a few fliers, and if this was the HQ building, it was much closer than the secured site had been. So even with his head start, Viridian might still find the drive before Chris/David did.

Flytrap was still active. She knew that if she went back to normal, she'd be a wreck of nerves. But hand to hand combat skills weren't very useful to her at the moment, so she reviewed the others and picked one.

Orchid

A bit of panic returned and her hands began to tremble. She forced herself to think, and the answers came quickly.

Amanda recalled Sasha's overt and abrupt attachment to her. She thought back to Ming, talking to them, and the way he'd gestured when he'd said "Y'all were security." It wasn't a half-hearted gesture, but one meant to encompass the both of them. Sasha's look right after had been one of fear, that Ming might have just clued Amanda in. She recalled Sasha's silence. At Ming's, it made sense. She didn't want to say something and have Ming react as if he recognized her. But why at the jewelry shop? She thought. The police had called Marcus about her. And he'd used femine pronouns to refer to the detective. She realized that the detective Marcus had spoken to must have been Sasha, trying to collect info on her.

She understood that she'd known Sasha before. Sasha was probably like her; a combat bot. She realized with a start that all the evidence pointed to her not having anything resembling a normal life prior to her memory loss. But Sasha had been a part of that life, an important part. And she'd felt betrayed by Amanda's efforts to collect that evidence. Amanda worried, given what she'd learned about the way she had manipulated Mike, if Sasha was right.

She supposed it didn't matter, now. She needed to look forward, and plan.

The drive contained evidence of something. Amanda had, indeed, been a Viridian employee, but she'd turned on the company and apparently agreed to deliver some sort of evidence to Chris/David and whomever he was working for. So finding that evidence first was the key. If she had it, she'd be in a position to negotiate with Viridian.

The problem was Sasha. Even after the attack at the secured site, Amanda wasn't willing to let her be killed, which Viridian would very likely do. In fact, all of Bob's talk about dealing with her and Sasha was probably just talk. The smart thing for Viridian to do would be to suck up whatever losses Amanda and Sasha's deaths would incur, to avoid history repeating itself in the future, once Amanda had re-established some trust within the company.

Amanda might have betrayed Sasha once, but was determined not to do so again.

If she went after the evidence, Sasha would be killed. But if she rescued Sasha, Viridian would find the evidence, at which point there wouldn't be any more constraints on their behavior, and they'd send everything they had after Sasha and her.

What she needed to do was either somehow guarantee that Chris/David would find the drive first, at which point Viridian would refocus on finding him, or do something to at least stall Viridian from killing Sasha. The latter was more tenable.

She switched her focus over the console display below the security feeds. It was asking for a biometric login. She glanced at the two guards, one dead, one bound and regaining consciousness. She couldn't trust the bound one, and she couldn't risk the biometric sensor registering that the other was dead and setting off an alarm.

Viridian was a huge company, and even their security division seemed to have multiple, independent departments. If Amanda had been running security, she'd have blocked and flagged her own biometrics immediately, and pushed it through to every other department as a priority one.

And those other departments would have done the same in their own time. She recalled Hornsby's words, 'DevSec agents'. She contrasted them with Bob's claim to be a part of White Team.

She found the reader and pressed her thumb to it. The display changed.

Welcome, Agent Aster.

Yes! She quickly began poking through the systems, looking for something she could use. There was a massive help resource; a veritable library of information about Viridian's networking protocols. She opened it up, and to her surprise, found she could read an entire screen's worth of text in an instant. She began flashing through screens as rapidly as she could, absorbing every word of the information. An idea formed.

She finished the document she had pulled up first, and then moved on to several others. By the time she finished the fourth, she had a plan. She had extremely high level clearance. She was blocked out of the DevSec network entirely, and she could see that a group task had been issued from it demanding that all other departments lock her out. But none of the other departments had marked the task as done. Browsing through prior tasks in the queue, she could see that they weren't flagged complete until all tagged departments had marked them done.

As expected, the private corporation cared a great deal about ticking the boxes, but significantly less about fostering inter-departmental cooperation. Good.

With basically unfettered access to everything but whatever DevSec was (she could find no documentation on the division other than a few memos reminding other departments that DevSec was an extremely high priority division with wide latitude to make demands of other departments, even when it impacted their own work), Amanda began digging around.

She quickly found a way to elevate her credentials, so she did so, getting executive level access. It still didn't get her into DevSec. Instead, she began flipping rapidly through informational screens, trying to figure out what was going on and how the company operated. She learned a lot. Their security apparatus, the so-called Spectrum Teams, were a combination of internal security and mercenary army. They'd done work for several other departments of the company, various cartels, powerful individuals and even taken government contracts. There were several flavors of teams: Blue Team were trigger-pullers, infantry teams. White Team was information and cyber security; tech geeks and spies-for-hire. Red Team was an assault force; heavy weapons and armored vehicles, including armed fliers and even a small space navy. Black Team was special operations; elite soldiers recruited from the best fighting units of all three nations on this planet.

One interesting fact she uncovered was that Rachel Hornsby had been placed in charge of DevSec, and had moved in on R&D shortly after she was hired, taking over its funding and executive operations. She couldn't get a clear picture of what happened with all the details blocked by DevSec, but she got the broad strokes from executive-level records. Two years after the internal takeover, R&D finished their work on the clonal tissue construction technique and Rachel Hornsby had been granted an executive vice-presidency in the Companion Production department.

By the time she was done researching, she had formed the nucleus of a plan. Amanda began composing memos and tasks and issuing them.

It took several minutes, by the end of which she could see that Sasha's interrogation had ended and she had been left on her own in the room. Like

Amanda, Sasha was crying, though she did so more quietly. The occasional tremble in her shoulders and the steady drip of tears onto her lap was the only evidence, with her head turned down the way it was.

But it was done. Amanda and Sasha were being held by White Team; the internal security and intelligence division. She'd put in orders to have Sasha transferred to a different site; an office building used predominantly by Viridian's security divisions. It was a secret location, technically owned by cutout companies which were themselves owned by yet more cutouts. It was also illegal as hell, with interrogation, destructive brain-scanning and holding facilities, even though the primary purpose was administration and logistics. Viridian would have closed it down, except it made for a convenient safehouse for any of their higher-ups or security agents who ran afoul of the law.

Emergency orders would come down from on high to transfer Sasha there, and the tasking Amanda had set up would ensure that she'd be all but forgotten, once transferred. White Team and Blue Team, the two departments Amanda knew would have knowledge of her, would be in the dark about her location and status. She'd set these orders to be released in twenty minutes, giving her plenty of time to get out and find transport. Other orders were set to be released in mere moments, giving her a distraction.

DevSec was a wildcard. Amanda didn't have the ability to prevent them from finding anything out, so she just had to hope for the best as far as they went. To tilt the odds in her favor, she logged into another system and began composing more orders. She set up an encryption system to keep her orders from being countermanded before they were fulfilled, and composed a key to that encryption that consisted of a couple hundred random characters which she herself would never remember, and they could never guess. Once done, she submitted her orders. That should buy her some time to escape, and hopefully keep DevSec occupied until it was too late.

With her work done, she quickly found the log files, erased her own tracks, then logged out.

`Flytrap`

It was time to go find that damned drive everyone wanted.

Aware

Wednesday, December 30th, 2759

Alarms blared and members of Blue Team - Viridian's trigger-pullers division- stomped through the halls in response. Employees of other departments hunkered down in their workspaces and waited for the all clear.

Gunfire rang out from the White Team building, followed by an explosion. Dozens of Blue Team soldiers converged on it, stacking up on doors and tossing in stun grenades before filing in. The whole structure was full of smoke and shouting men. Confusion reigned, and six Blue Team personnel and three White Team employees were killed in friendly-fire incidents. Two of the latter looked, rather strangely, to have been dead before the fighting broke out. Bob Han and Clarence Darrowman, White Team Interrogators.

Eventually, the responders got their shit together and cleared the building room by room. They found the prisoner; one of the DevSec commanders, bound to a chair in an interrogation room. They found the monitoring station and the dead guard, but there was no sign of his partner.

Eventually, Blue Team 4 found him, bound and gagged in the flier garage, stuffed into an equipment locker. When they got his gag off, he told them how the other DevSec commander had refused to cooperate under interrogation, escaped and killed his partner. How she'd knocked him out, bound him, and then vanished for several minutes. How she had returned, seized him and carried him to the flier garage, forcing him to open the launch doors using his biometrics, and then stuffed him in the locker.

Blue Team 4 checked the flight logs and found nothing. They checked the security feeds, and found a gap in the coverage. They dug around through White Team's network for a while, looking for any trace of the escaped prisoner, and then they found it.

In the combat bot control systems. But they found it too late.

Sixteen combat bots, very similar to the patrol bots used by the police, but more heavily armed and armored, and with the Viridian stylized V logo in place of a badge, came streaming into the flier garage, weapons firing. The Blue Team members there fought back, but there were only eight of them, and the bots had better aim.

They managed to knock out four of the bots before the last Blue Team guard was gunned down. The remaining twelve bots then joined the sixteen who had run around firing their guns into the ceiling, setting off the alarms before systemically sweeping the building again, following orders to kill everyone but the prisoner. When they finished, they moved on to the main HQ building, engaging the rest of Blue Team.

The fighting was fierce. It went on for forty two minutes. The police, already on edge after the prior shooting, responded quickly, but they were massively outgunned by both sides. They worked mostly to prevent any spillover, while letting Viridian handle its own rebelling bots.

Blue Team numbered in the hundreds, and the conclusion was foregone from the beginning. Twenty-eight bots just didn't stand a chance. But taking over the building wasn't their goal. The fight had been.

By the time anyone with any sway in the company thought to question what had happened to the other prisoner, Amanda was long gone.

Blue Team finally secured Sasha, who'd sat, confused and alone in her room throughout the entire ordeal, and then the specific group that found her followed the orders they'd been issued over the network, packing her into a flier and taking her out to their secret site for holding.

They'd been promised a week's PTO, to kick in as soon as they dropped her off, and all of them were eager to take it.

Amanda didn't remember if she knew how to drive a flier. But Flytrap apparently did. It was a strange sensation, using the entirely unfamiliar controls by instinct. But she managed to take off and get through the launch doors that way. By the time she sat the flier down on an empty lot half a block from where she'd woken up several nights before, she'd noted what all the gauges and readouts meant, and what all the controls did. It was a sort of learning on fast-forward.

Chris/David should be around here somewhere. Hopefully, Viridian would take a while to get someone out after the chaos she'd left them in. She kept her eyes peeled as she made her way to the building she had woken up behind, uncomfortable in her stolen guard's uniform.

She approached it from the front. It was an eight-story, red-brick structure with a grid of windows. The entrance was a glass foyer, with the street number glowing above the door in a holo display. She stopped when she got there.

There was blood on the stoop, shining in the blue glow from the street lights.

A pair of dark red rings. Crusted blood outlined where two small puddles had dried out. No-one had cleaned it up, only the footsteps of residents and visitors worked to erase them. Amanda wondered whose blood it was. Probably hers.

She walked in and changed state codes.

`Orchid`

She immediately connected to the building management network and flashed random passwords at it until it accepted one. She knew, without knowing how, that they always relented after no more than a few seconds. Inevitably, one of the residents would have a stupid password.

She found the leasing directory and looked for anyone named Nash, finding him after a moment. Unit 603, sixth floor. She walked to the stairwell, saw another bloodstain there, and turned back to take the elevator.

She didn't know why it disturbed her so much, but it did.

She waited for the lift to descend, boarded it and rode it up to the sixth floor. She stepped off and followed the public signs through dirty halls that smelled of urine and mildew.

Apartment 603 has a police holo in front of the door, but no-one was around. The door itself was missing, a few splinters hanging off the hinges telling the story of where it went. She stepped through the holo and into the apartment. It was the same one from the footage she had seen.

She stepped to the table, where she found more dried blood. A few red and black hairs were embedded in the blood at one end. The blood on the other end still held the faint outline of Nash's head and arm. She moved on, approaching the window.

Her heart twisted at the mess below it. Dried blood, still chunky with bits of drying brain tissue and splinters of bone. The Orchid state code wasn't like Flytrap. She could still feel everything, it was just a bit muted. Her vision swam with tears as she replayed the footage she'd watched in her heads up display.

Mike's words rang out. "Please, remember where you left the thing, babe. When you wake up, just grab it and go. I love you, Amanda."

The last four words stabbed straight into her heart and embedded themselves there with a bitter, painful impact.But her mind seized on the words before it. "Just grab it and go." Wherever it was, it was close to where Mike had left her.

She pushed the window open and looked out onto the alleyway where she'd woken up. The spot she'd woken up wasn't directly below the window. In fact, the dumpster was between the ground below the window and the spot she'd woken up in. She recalled the way he'd leaned out the window as he threw her.

He was guiding her. Towards what, though?

She eyed the scene from the same perspective Mike would have. The only thing that made sense was the dumpster. He'd wanted her to be on the other side of the dumpster.

Amanda turned and quickly left the apartment. She ran down the stairs and circled around, coming to the alley from the street the young men who'd startled her had been walking down. Examining the ground, she found another bloodstain.

She moved to the dumpster, patting her gun belt and finding a small flashlight in a pouch there. She clicked it on and began looking around. She saw a disturbance on the ground where she had landed. Nothing about the dumpster stood out to her, despite pouring over the exterior for several minutes. She even shined the flashlight through the struts on the bottom and sides of the dumpster, but saw nothing inside.Finally, she opened the lid.

In order to see better, she climbed the wall and hopped inside. Bags of trash overflowed it still, reassuring her that it hadn't been emptied. She pushed bags out until she saw something go skittering into the corner.

Amanda tossed most of the rest of the bags out of the dumpster and then grabbed the bag the thing had slid under and pushed it behind her. There it was. A small 'thumb drive'. It was a modern take on an ancient design; a scant few dozen terabytes of storage on an unpowered chip. It needed to be plugged into a system with an appropriate connector on it to work. It was outdated, archaic technology whose very obsolescence made it perfect for this sort of thing. It couldn't be tracked or scanned for easily, and it was exactly the sort of thing that could go overlooked, even if found.

She stuck it quickly in a pocket with a cover and sealed it. Climbing out of the dumpster, she was startled by a voice behind her.

"I've got a gun aimed right at your asshole, and if I pull this trigger, you're gonna hurt real bad for a long time, and then die, understand?"

She froze, but the voice was familiar.

"Da-I mean Chris?"

She peeked carefully behind her, and sure enough, it was him. True to his word, he was pointing a vicious-looking handgun at her rear.

"Shit, Amanda? What the fuck are you doing here?" He put his gun away in the small of his back.

"They raided your secured site, earlier tonight. I've been in Viridian custody for a few hours."

"You have got to be… Shit." Chris/David winced and slammed a fist into his own leg in frustration. "Fuck, they must have followed me with a sat or an orbiter or something. Something I couldn't see."

He glanced around the alley as if a solution to this problem might present itself. Nothing did, of course. His eyes came to rest on Amanda, and she saw a bit of concern darken his features.

"Where's your friend?" he asked.

"She…" Amanda didn't know what to say. "She knew me from… From before. When you left, she attacked me. She was crying, saying that I lied to her… I-"

"Shit, she must not have known about your deal…"

"My deal?"

"Your deal with us. In exchange for the evidence, you made us promise to get you off the planet and to the Empire, get you a new identity and a modest bank account, and to do the same for two others."

Amanda went a little weak at the knee with relief. "I was going to take her. Her and Mike," she exclaimed as a heavy load of guilt shifted off of her shoulders. She hadn't realized just how much that guilt had been weighing on her until she heard this, and she found herself breathing heavily at the sudden change. Even the state code she was riding couldn't suppress her excitement.

She hadn't betrayed either of them. She'd been trying to save them!

"Yeah, I guess that was the fucking plan… Until it wasn't."

"What do you mean?" she asked, still reeling from the last revelation.

"I mean I should have fucking gone with you and your boyfriend. Cindy didn't want me to, said somebody other than the lords of the rings needed to do overwatch. Shit, for everything that went wrong, I was sitting there, twiddling my damned thumbs on a channel with Cindy while the others breathed down my neck. I fucking *knew* I should have gone. Hell, I should have brought the other two, had them escort you in, instead of letting your boyfriend do it. Shit."

"Who's Cindy?" Amanda asked. Her mind was racing, trying to game the situation. She still wasn't sure where she stood with him. She carefully made no moves towards the pocket that contained the drive. It gave her leverage, as long as she held onto it, but Chris/David might try to take it if he found out. She could always call Flytrap, but so far, she'd only fought normal humans with it, and she strongly suspected that Chris/David and whoever Cindy was might be Draughtgen. She wasn't sure exactly why, but the notion gnawed at the back of her mind.

"Gods, this amnesia thing gets old," he spat. As he noticed Amanda narrowing her eyes at him, he quickly added "I know it's not your fault. It's just frustrating. Alright, let me tell you what I know, okay?

"Cindy is my partner. She was your driver, the day you snatched the evidence. The idea was to be as low-profile as possible. You and your boyfriend would go in to work, like any other day. He would use your credentials to pull the data we needed to prove what they're up to, while you went and got your friend out of there. I don't know exactly what your deal was, but I got some pretty strong love triangle vibes.

"I don't know exactly what went wrong. I was still in touch with Cindy when the silent alarms went off. They went to the company's security division, not to the cops, so the reaction was quick. It was maybe one minute from the time the alarms tripped until you two came running out of the building, security hot on your heels. You made it to the car, only a little worse for wear, and Cindy took off, but they got an armed flier on you. I sent the other two out to intercept it, but it managed to make a gun run before they took it out. It tore the vehicle up, something fierce.

You were injured, having seizures and unable to talk. Cindy told me you seemed awake and aware, but having trouble communicating. Your boyfriend had snatched some parts before you guys came out. I guess just for the extra evidence though he said they could use them to fix your damage. So he had her take you to a guy he knew who could supposedly fix you. Guess he should have picked a better guy. In any event, Cindy was supposed to give them time to work, then pick you back up. But when she returned, she found the place crawling with armed men. Mercenaries, on contract to Viridian to supplement their own security force. Some of the same guys were following me around, but I think I lost them after our little run-in at the jewelry shop."

"I killed them," Amanda said quietly, remembering the three men at the unfinished office building. "Three of them, at least."

Chris/David nodded. "And I got two more at the shop. I guess with a third of their men dead in one night, they decided to cut their losses."

They stood in silence for a moment while Amanda went over this new knowledge, and tried to decide what to do with it. Eventually, she settled on a plan.

"I know where the drive is," Amanda said.

"What?" Chris/David's eyebrows shot up. "I thought you didn't-"

"I figured it out. I don't remember, exactly, but I found out some things while they were interrogating me. Hell, they told me more than they even asked me. They showed me security camera footage. Seems like a dumb mistake for interrogators, but they were legitimately trying to convince me to cooperate. I guess the appearance of being forthright was more valuable than withholding information from me."

"Okay, well, where is it?"

Amanda shook her head. "Not that easy. I still need to get Sasha. I had her moved somewhere that it will be easier to break her free from. I need your help to go get her."

Chris/David stared at her for a moment, shaking his head slowly. "Amanda, you may not remember this, but the evidence on that drive is literally a matter of life and death-"

"I don't care." Amanda interrupted. "I don't give a shit, Chris. Or David. Whoever the fuck you are. I am going to get her, and if you want that fucking drive, you'll help me."

He eyed her from under lowered brows for another moment. The silence dragged out until he broke it with an exaggerated sigh.

"Fine. Whatever. But I'm bringing you to Cindy, first. She's leading this op, and she's the one who's been working with you."

He headed out the mouth of the alley. Amanda followed, but stopped as she turned onto the street. She looked back and up, to the slightly-cracked window Mike had thrown her through. She imagined the mess on the other side, and then imagined Mike, slumped over on the floor in front of the window. Her vision went blurry again, the State code unable to hold back the tide of grief.

"Goodbye, Mike. I'm so sorry for…" She took a deep, shuddering breath. "I love you, too."

Chris/David drove her again, but this time, they went downtown. He took her through the commercial district where she'd outfitted herself two days ago. It was mostly closed down at the moment with relatively few people on the sidewalks, but the nightlife district nearby was crowded and lively. He rode the accelerator like a drowning man would ride a log raft, but when traffic got tight, he didn't express any frustration. He simply watched, constantly, periodically checking a device he had pulled out of the center console and placed on the dash.

"What is that?" Amanda asked.

"Surveillance scanner. If they've got a camera pointed at us, even from orbit, this thing will give me a bearing and distance to it. I'm looking for anything that stands out, like something straight above us, or coming from eye level on the streets. Lots of traffic and security cameras, so it takes a lot of checking to know if I should be concerned."

He drove to The Towers, a district full of nicer residential buildings, and then into the garage attached to the White Lotus building; the tallest structure in the city. Amanda accessed her BCI and began reading about the building's storied history. It was a landmark, and one of the most famous buildings in the city. Surprisingly, it was not that expensive to live there.

The White Lotus had been built as luxury apartments, right as the culture in New Kowloon had experienced a shift some four decades back. The ultra wealthy -the targeted demographic- began to flock to Manyan province -then a slum being parceled off for demolition- and buy large tracts of land upon which to build grand palaces. The White Lotus had fallen on hard times almost as soon as it opened, and the companies that built it almost all went bankrupt. The banks owned it, but even they didn't want it. So stakes were sold off to those few buyers they found, with the hope of offsetting the considerable maintenance bills onto those buyers.

This drove down the prices to the point that organized crime took note of the building's state-of-the-art security, low prices, out-and-out ownership and realized what a prime opportunity it afforded. By the end of the White Lotus's first decade, it was owned almost entirely by a coalition of cartels, nominally called the Community Coalition, but widely referred to as Cartel Squared. The remaining stakes were held by private individuals, mostly part of the wealthy elite, but unable to afford the now-astronomical price tag associated with a move to Manyan province. None had the power to influence the cartels, and indeed, it was the cartels who influenced them, absorbing their modest fortunes and making room for them within their ranks.

The structure quickly developed a reputation for lawlessness. The whole city knew it as the place to go to buy drugs and illegal media, hire hitmen and thugs and just rub elbows with the edgy, criminal underground. A famous viral video, twenty five years old now, showed two men openly carrying a dead body through the lobby, utterly unconcerned about witnesses, including the man filming them, for whom they had stopped to pose with their victim for a couple of stills. To this day, no-one has identified the body or the men involved.

By the end of the second decade, the film and serial makers had taken note of the place's emerging reputation. Soon, crime dramas began to feature the place. The cartels in turn took notice, and built studios to siphon money out of the filmmakers. This, in turn, attracted a different kind of low-life, in the form of lawyers, agents and fixers, all of whom either actively sought out, or else simply didn't mind the association with organized crime.

The White Lotus's reputation had become a self-fulfilling prophecy that only grew over the years. Multiple attempts to clean it up -including one just this year, by the new provisional government- had failed. Its status as a zone of urban lawlessness had grown too powerful; the public, along with all the resources the cartels could bring to bear were set against any such attempt. The White Lotus was a place where a disgruntled employee could find a man to intimidate his boss, where powerful politicians could go to have their rivals removed, and where aspiring actors, musicians and other entertainers could go to begin or grow their careers.

In short, it was the perfect place for a spy to set up shop.

Chris/David walked her through teeming crowds of people visiting the countless twenty-four hour businesses. Film crews, tattooed gangsters, mafioso in expensive suits, shady lawyers in cheap suits and thousands upon thousands of tourists filled the lower levels and rode with them up dozens of elevator landings. They shared their elevator with others all the way up to the 50th floor. After that, they rode in silence up to the 193rd floor; the top.

They got off and Chris/David led her down three different halls to a corner apartment. Once there, he engaged in an elaborate ritual. He pulled two different key fobs from his pockets and clicked them. He knocked on the door, three precisely-spaced raps, then he stared at the security plate over the access panel. It slid back and he pushed in a code she couldn't see. She heard the lock on the door click open and took a step forward.

"Not!" Chris/David shouted, startling her into immobility.

"Yet," he finished in a more reasonable tone.

He took a step back and Amanda copied him. The door opened to reveal a short, heavily muscled older man with a thick, black beard and eyes that were simultaneously dead and oh-so hungry. A chill ran through her and she resisted the urge to switch to Flytrap. This man was a killer, more so than anyone else she'd encountered thus far.

"Who's your friend?" the man rumbled.

"You don't recognize her?" Chris/David asked.

"'Course I do. Don't understand why you brought one here, though. Mighty fucking suspicious, you ask me."

"She's not a Seven series, she's-" Chris/David started to explain, but Amanda spoke up for herself.

"You want the fucking drive? Let me the fuck in."

The man grinned at her, a sight even more terrifying than his scowl had been. Amanda's BCI warned her that the threat assessment had reached seventy eight percent, but she ignored it.

"You heard the lady, Gimli," Chris/David said.

The gruff face relaxed a bit and he pushed the door open for them. As she followed Chris/David in, she could see that he held a rifle in the same hand he held the door with. Inside the spacious apartment, another man waited for them. This one was tall and thin, with a gaunt face and equally haunted eyes. He regarded Amanda impassively as Chris/David approached him.

"Cindy awake yet?" he asked the man. A nod was his only response. Chris/David nodded back and then glanced at Amanda. "Amanda, this is Legolas. Legolas, this is our inside man, Amanda."

"Amanda," he said and gave her a nod.

Gimli and Legolas. The names sounded familiar, but she couldn't place them.

She followed Chris/David into the room, and found a woman sitting on the edge of the bed. She had no shirt on, and her abdomen was wrapped in clean bandages. She had a model's face and build; tall, thin and busty with delicate, patrician features. Amanda didn't recognize her at all. Not even a slight sense of familiarity.

"Amanda," the woman said with a warm smile, "I'm so glad you made it. David told us he'd found you."

"He told me his name was Chris," Amanda responded.

"He didn't recognize you, Amanda. You two had never met before he ran into you at the jewelry store."

Amanda looked at David, who shrugged. "I was right," she said. "About your name, I mean."

"Yes. I told you to find him, before I dropped you and Mike off at that building. Right before you lost consciousness." Cindy patted the bed and Amanda sat. David took a chair.

"Are you in a behavioral state now, Amanda?"

Amanda debated lying, but decided against it. "Yes."

"Which one?"

"Orchid."

Cindy thought for a second. "That's tradecraft, right?" Amanda nodded.

"Can you turn it off?"

"I don't know if I trust you enough to turn it off."

Cindy picked up a tablet off the bed and tapped it. A holorecording scene began to play on it. She saw herself, dressed in workout clothes, sitting on a wooden chair at a wooden table. It was the same wooden table Legolas had been sitting at, in one of the chairs surrounding it.

"I'm not sure how I'm supposed to do this," the recorded version of herself said.

"Just start at the beginning." The voice belonged to Cindy.

"Okay. Do I need to swear an oath or something?"

"If you want to. You don't need to, though. We just need a record of your testimony, to establish the provenance of the evidence."

"Okay. Um, My name is Amanda. Amanda Aster. I am a bot, constructed with a sapient mind by Viridian Dynamics' military arms division under contract to the government of the People's Republic of Arthesia, at that time headed by Prime Minister General Covington.

"My mind is modeled on a Calanthi-Peterson matrix; a mathematical model of-"

Cindy turned the recording off.

"Wait," Amanda said. "I need to see that!"

Cindy nodded. "Yes, and you will, I promise. But I need to speak to Amanda. Not the Orchid behavioral state."

Amanda eyed her. She weighed the pros and cons. One the one hand, it would help establish a rapport. On the other hand, she would be more susceptible to manipulation. Amanda weighed the choices and decided to risk it. If Cindy asked about the drive, she'd switch back in an instant and try to disguise the change.

Daisy

The collected stress hit her like a ton of bricks, and she sobbed before she could stop herself. An image of the guard whose throat she had stomped swam up in her mind's eye, and she felt like she was going to be sick.

Cindy put an arm around her shoulder. "I know, I know. You've been through so much."

Amanda allowed the woman to hold her for a minute before pulling away and taking a deep, shuddering breath. The Orchid state code didn't mute emotions the way Flytrap did, so she'd expected an easier time transitioning back to normal, but it hadn't been easy at all. She had needed a moment, but she was fine now.

"Okay, so what do you want to talk about," Amanda asked.

"Tell me everything you remember."

Amanda laughed bitterly. "I remember waking up in an alley. I was filthy, covered in blood and bruises. The only things I remembered at that point was my first name, and two more. David and Mike. I knew Mike was important. I knew I needed to find David. That's it."

Cindy nodded and glanced at David. He nodded back. "And your friend, Sasha. You have no memory of her from before that?"

"I don't remember *anything* before that."

"Then how did you find her? She wasn't one of the names."

"She found me. She tracked me after things went wrong, stealing the drive. She… She killed an informant she had and took her place. Pretended to flirt with me in a makeup shop, gave me her phone number. After I met David, some men captured me and tried to interrogate me about him, but I escaped and killed them. I didn't know what else to do, so I called the only person I knew."

Cindy nodded. "That's remarkably good tradecraft. She tracked you, predicted your moves and got herself in position for you to come to her. She knew, or deduced what condition you would be in, and knew how to ingratiate herself with you. So where is she?"

"Sasha…" Amanda took a steadying breath. "She attacked me at the secured site, just after David left."

"Did she say anything?"

"She told me I lied, that I lied about everything. She told me I had trusted her, until I didn't. She was manic, almost. Barely coherent."

"Sudden, overwhelming emotions are a common problem with sapient AIs. The human mind is easy to replicate on an individual basis, but very difficult to recreate perfectly from the ground up. Even the most advanced human-like AIs like yours can experience them. There's a treatment, you know. It's close to a hundred percent effective. Not quite there, but the chances that we can help your friend are very good."

Amanda nodded.

"So what happened to her?" Cindy asked.

"Viridian tracked us. They took us. I escaped, but she's still being held. I'm going to get her."

Cindy nodded, as if Amanda's declaration was obvious and expected. She turned to David, who nodded to her. "Secured site's charges went off last night, just a few minutes after I left. I didn't see the blast for the trees, but every charge went off, according to the sensors. We lost the site, but that's it. Viridian probably lost a few guys based on spectral lines in the flames. Lots more organics than there should have been."

Cindy turned back to Amanda. "So now I suppose our deal has changed. Instead of getting you and two other people off planet and set up in the Empire, you want us to help you rescue your friend, and then get the two of you off planet."

Amanda shrugged. "I'm going to get her, either way. If you want the drive, you can help."

Cindy looked at David, who stood and walked over to her. With a sudden movement, as fast as a striking snake, he snatched the pocket off her stolen jacket, taking the drive with it.

Amanda shot to her feet, ready to turn on Flytrap, but David held up his hands in a defensive gesture. "No need to go hot. We're still gonna help, Amanda."

Cindy waved a hand to get Amanda's attention. "We'll help. We just need to secure that evidence. You can trust us."

Amanda looked back and forth, her eyes wide. They'd just removed her leverage, but promised to cooperate anyways. She didn't know what else she could do, so she nodded warily and sat back down.

Cindy shot David a meaningful look, then called out "Hey boys! Come on in here."

Legolas entered first, carrying a rifle almost as long as he was, Gimli hot on his heels. Gimli took a seat next to Amanda and Legolas took the last chair.

"Alright, Amanda. Tell us what you can about where Sasha is."

Amanda looked around. She didn't trust anyone in this room, the two armed men least of all. Both looked like the kind to slaughter innocents and talk about 'unfortunate damages' after the fact. And David and Cindy… She'd been working with them, but that didn't mean she had trusted them before.

But they were all she had. And truth be told, if they played straight with her, she was now in the best position possible, by having allies who were helping of their own free wills. Well, short of living happily ever after with Mike and Sasha. She sighed, realizing she had no other option. But before she spoke…

`Orchid`

Amanda considered how much to tell them. Honestly, she realized the state code wasn't really helping, because she had so little choice here. They already had the drive, and she was at their mercy, if she wanted their help.

"I forged orders to have her transferred to a less physically secure site. When I escaped, I caused enough chaos to keep them running around blind for a while. We've got maybe twelve hours -more like ten, now- before someone notices that she's gone, figures out where she's gone to and gets her back under enough protection to make the rescue unfeasible."

Amanda pulled a map up in her heads up display and looked at the tablet. "Does that thing have a projector?"

"Of course," Cindy said, and stood to place it on a desk, carefully pointing the top at the far wall. Amanda focused on it and sent the map over as a stream. The tablet lit up the wall with it, and she zoomed in on some skyscrapers in a commercial district near downtown.

"The site is here," she said, highlighting one of the shorter buildings. "It's a secret site, owned through a number of cutouts, and used by Viridian's security apparatus. It has holding cells, but it's not a containment facility, it's mostly used for administrative stuff, and as a place to hide security agents who run afoul of law enforcement. But they also run some less-than-legal activities through there, from time to time."

She replaced the map with a schematic of the building. A 3d view swirled, one section on the twelfth floor highlighted. "This is where they will be keeping her. There's only about fifty to eighty guards there at any given time. If we hit them right at dawn, that number should be closer to fifty. That's… That's as much as I have planned. Maybe I did this stuff all the time before, but I don't remember how, now. If it was just me, I was going to wing it."

Gimli whistled. "Attacking a secure facility with fifty armed guards ain't exactly the time you want to wing it, darling."

Amanda glanced at him. She was torn between snapping at him not to call her 'darling' and just letting it slide to avoid pissing him off. He was probably Draughtgen, too. Which meant that Flytrap might not be enough. She should let it slide.

"That's why I'm here, shortstack. I'm hoping I won't have to."

Apparently, Orchid didn't let things slide easily.

Legolas threw his head back and laughed in a surprisingly deep voice. "She's got your number, Gimli," he said. Gimli didn't seem offended though, grinning at her through his beard. "Yeah, you're fun," he said.

"So what kind of plan can you suggest, boys?" Cindy asked. "You're our tactical experts, after all."

Gimli looked at Legolas, who nodded to him. Gimli nodded back before turning to face Cindy.

"Go in through the front, shoot every motherfucker in the way, grab the target, walk out."

"And how," David asked, leaning forward, "Is that any better than winging it?"

Gimli grinned again. "Because I've got six suits of Berserker in a cache just about three klicks from that building." David grinned back. Legolas lounged in his chair and looked bored. Cindy's eyebrows rose and Amanda frowned in confusion. "What's Berserker?"

Angry

Wednesday, December 30th, 2759

As it turned out, Berserker was a powered-exoskeletal, full-enclosure combat armor system used as the standard infantry armor by the Imperial Defense Force. It was a metal suit, ranging from two to eight centimeters thick, the outside coated in a matte black rubbery substance. It had no face, no markings, and the only distinguishing features were small cylindrical protuberances scattered around the shoulders, hips, upper arms and legs. Inside each protuberance were the characteristic fan blades of tiny, high-powered jet engines.

Gimli gave her a crash course on the armor as they drove. The weight of four armored people in the cargo van they'd had stashed in the White Lotus parking garage made it ride very low on the suspension. The motors whined at the strain at first, but Cindy simply engaged the percussion drive and they managed to get up to speed amidst the dull clattering of the drive hammers.

"There's a lot of systems in this armor. Unfortunately, active camouflage isn't one of them. The ones you need to concern yourself with are the weapons interface, the status display and the self-repair systems. Grab that rifle, and I'll show you the weapons interface."

Amanda picked up a rifle from the stack of them in the center of the van, and a readout appeared on her HUD. The armor seemed super advanced for military tech (which she instinctively knew tended to be a ways back from the state-of-the-art, for reliability reasons). The faceplate was solid steel, yet once she closed it up, the inside had simply vanished, giving her a clear field of view. The elements of the HUD occupied the corners of her vision, and instantly centered themselves whenever she tried to focus on one, popping right back to her peripheral view when she stopped.

Once powered up, the armor barely seemed to weigh anything, thanks to the power-assist movement features. Despite having to strip and coat herself in a sticky-yet-slimy gel in order to get in, it felt a lot like wearing a soft, satin jumpsuit. To her surprise, she could feel sensations through the armored gauntlets and even the rest of the suit. An itch had begun between her shoulder blades after she suited up, and she instinctively rubbed her back against a doorframe, surprising herself when it actually worked. David had shown her how to get the armor to scratch any itches itself, and that helped keep her sane for the first few minutes as her body reacted to being enclosed by popping up itches all over the place, particularly where she'd been injured.

The armor also had medical systems which had dispatched drugs and even medical nanites to the wound on her leg. She hadn't realized how much it still hurt until the suit had flashed "administering analgesic" in the HUD and the burning ache had gone away.

Gimli walked her through how to use the armor's HUD to aim her weapon or peer down the barrel camera between rounds, how to engage and disengage the aiming assist and how to use the ammo counter. Amanda paid close attention, and was relieved at how intuitive and familiar this all seemed. She knew she couldn't be getting her memories back, but she also knew that a lot of combat skills were still there, and the instincts they forged would help.

She held off on changing state codes until the shooting started, however. Except for the last time, she'd immediately launched into violence upon changing states to Flytrap, and on that occasion, she had still run towards the remaining guards in the building to kill. She wasn't sure if she would attack the others, and she didn't want to take the chance.

After she demonstrated enough proficiency to satisfy Gimli, he went over the status display, which basically just told her what was operational and not in the armor. That only took a moment. Finally, he showed her how to direct the self-repair systems to prioritize repairs that would assist her tactical goals. That too, went quickly, and by the time he finished, they had turned onto the road the security site fronted and were heading towards it.

The building was a concrete box with a grid of plate glass windows. It lacked even the most basic of decorative touches.

"When we get there," Gimli said, "Cindy is not going to stop. We're going to open the rear door and use the thrusters on the armor to brake ourselves right out the back."

"You didn't show me how to use the thrusters!" Amanda objected.

"They're slaved to me, you don't need to do anything. I'm just letting you know what's going to happen."

"Wait, how do I-" Amanda was interrupted by the rear doors flying open, her armor roughly turning with her inside to face it and the cylinders on her back and legs shifting their angles and emitting a dense plume of hot gasses.

She flew out the back along with the other two, the jets spinning her around and flaring up to deposit her on her feet, directly in front of the building. Gimli and Legolas were already rushing in, firing rapidly at the guards at the front, who shot back ineffectually with handguns.

Flytrap

Amanda followed them in, right behind David. Just as she passed a corridor leading back, she saw a flash of motion out of the corner of her eye and her HUD drew a threatening silhouette of running figures over the wall that quickly blocked her view.

She stopped and turned, dropping to one knee and raising the rifle. As the knot of guards emerged, she opened fire. The rifle didn't bang the way she expected it to, making instead a loud clack-crack sound with each round. The bullets tore through the guards as she stood, walking sideways to pie the corner and ensure she got all of them.

One in the back got a shot off, but it spanked off her armor, feeling like nothing more than a pebble bouncing off of her.

When they were all down, she checked her schematic. There were elevators down this corridor, and another bank down a similar corridor on the other side of the reception desk. She toggled the radio in the armor and said "Frag out," before aiming the underbarrel attachment of her rifle at the floor selector in between the two sets of doors and triggering a round from it.

This weapon made a loud "ploomp" sound as it fired and she quickly ducked around the corner as the loud blast and shockwave washed out.

She heard Legolas repeat her warning a split second later, and another loud crack shook the building. That was both banks, according to the schematic. She turned towards the others to see Gimli already stacking up on the stairwell door, David behind him. Legolas positioned himself and Amanda brought up the rear.

"Straight up," Gimli said, "Ignore the other floors. They might come from below us, but that's better than getting bogged down trying to clear eleven floors of this place while they just lock down and call in backup."

As soon as he finished speaking, he kicked open the door and rushed in. Amanda followed Legolas at a steady pace, and quickly found herself running up flights of stairs lit by pale fluorescent lights. A cracking, whooshing sound began to emanate from behind her, and the status display indicated that the thrusters on her armor were firing to help propel her up the stairs. She took them five at a time, bounding easily up each flight in two steps.It took very little time to reach the twelfth floor, marked by large numbers on the wall of the landing in glowing illumipaint.

Gimli stopped next to the door, and they stacked up behind him in the same order as last time. "Right, then left,alternating," he said over the radio, then counted down from three.

He kicked the door and ran in, gunfire erupting almost immediately. Amanda heard rounds smacking into the walls and pinging off of armor as David rushed in, cutting left. Legolas went right with Gimli, so she darted through and followed David.

It was a large office floor, with cubicle dividers that stood chest high dividing the room into a labyrinthine mess of tiny squares and short halls. At least two dozen faces of Blue Team soldiers were in evidence, peering above and around the dividers behind the barrels of assault rifles spitting fire at them. Two, three, five rounds skipped off her armor. She kept about three meters between David and her, as they moved all the way left to the exterior wall, then turned towards the far end, where the holding cells were.

She kept her rifle up, spitting rounds towards the enemy. The heads up display kept a glowing white crosshair up wherever her weapon was aimed, so she didn't even have to acquire a sight picture to fire for effect. As they turned the corner, she noted movement as more men rushed in. A bad feeling was beginning to form in her guts when she heard Gimli shout "Everyone back to the stairwell!"

She froze for just a second, not understanding why he'd call a retreat. She looked over to see Legolas standing tall, his weapon on the floor, his helmet rocking left and right as he cracked his neck. Rounds spanked off his armor, but he ignored them.

David had backpedaled as soon as Gimli transmitted. "Come on!" He said to Amanda, "We need to get behind Legolas, let's go."

"Why?" Amanda asked as she turned to follow him back.

"Berserker," he gasped.

"What?" Amanda didn't understand why he was mentioning the armor.

"Not the armor, hun," Gimli said as they joined him. "Combat Dissociative State. Legolas is an actual berserker. He's going to clear the room for us."

A sudden roar shook the cubicle dividers and startled her. It was Legolas, screaming through his external speakers. As she watched, he rushed forward, unarmed.

Amanda's jaw might have dropped even further, had not the chin of her helmet held it up. She'd never seen anyone move so fast, she hadn't even known it was possible. Legolas laid into them with his bare hands, silvery blades extending from his gauntlets as he literally tore the enemy limb from limb.

Blood splattered the walls and cubicles. A window shattered as one man was thrown straight through the nominally bulletproof glass. The tiny size of the window hadn't been an impediment, because the man had no legs left.

She couldn't even keep track of the violence, it was happening so fast and involved so much blood. Even in her Flytrap state, the gore and screaming twisted her stomach and she had to clamp down to avoid vomiting in her helmet. That would be bad. But she couldn't take her eyes off the whirlwind of body parts and blood, and the armored figure in its eye.

It took no more than fifteen or twenty seconds for the chaos to come to a conclusion. Whimpering, mewling and screaming continued, as the movement stopped. Legolas stood still in the middle of the carnage, and she could see his shoulders heaving as he breathed heavily. He stood motionless for a few more seconds, then drew the sidearm from the holster on his leg and began to put the survivors out of their misery. That too, was over quickly, and then silence reigned.

Less than a minute after it started, Legolas walked back in his blood soaked armor to retrieve his rifle.

"Room clear," he announced in a calm voice, and Gimli actually laughed over the radio. Amanda shook her head and bit her own tongue, appalled that someone could be so callous as to laugh at that level of violence.

They moved forward, still on guard in case more enemies appeared.

The door the guards had been coming through led to a hall with regular doors on either side. Amanda knew from the schematic that most of these rooms held middle-management offices. At the end of the hall, they encountered a steel door embedded in a thick plasticrete wall.

David moved forward, pulling a cable from his armored forearm and sticking the small pad at the end to the center of the door. That done, he retrieved a vial from the built-in backpack in his armor and slotted the notched end into the accommodating notch on the pad.

Silver metal flowed out of the pad and vanished into the cracks in the door, leaving behind tiny hair-thin wires connecting them back. David crouched, unmoving and Amanda realized he was hacking the systems. That cable and vial seemed quite useful.

It took a minute or two, but eventually, she heard a few muted thuds and the metal reappeared, flowing out of the cracks and back towards the pad. David waited for it all to return and then stowed his gear and stepped back. Gimli took his place, and they stacked up. This time, David took the last slot while Amanda rested her hand on Legolas' back.

With another countdown, Gimli pushed the door open and rushed in. Legolas, Amanda and David followed. It was another corridor, this one with thick plasticrete walls and exposed metal beams. The doors lining it were farther apart and had exterior locks and small windows in them, except for the first door on the right.

Amanda went directly to that door while the others continued down the hall, Legolas and David checking the windows in the doors while Gimli proceeded straight forward to the T intersection at the end.

She gently tried the handle and found it locked. Remembering David's trick, she focused on the status display and found the same port on her forearm with the stored cable. She unlocked it, sending the command through her BCI, then reached into the storage compartment on her back, which opened automatically as her hand approached. She dug around carefully and found a vial.

She copied David's actions, and then scrolled through the functions associated with the cable until she found one called "Smart Metal Interface". Flowing liquid metal that went where it was most useful seemed pretty smart to her, so she tried it.

The display in her field of view changed to a 3D model of the door with her gear stuck to it. She used the eyeblink controls that popped up, hitting "Deploy smart metal", which resulted in the metal flowing out and into the cracks. A new menu appeared, and one of the options it provided was "Automatic Door Unlock". She chose that and waited while the 3D model did things she didn't understand, rotating and zooming and panning around.

After just twenty seconds or so, a green light lit up and the model zoomed back out. She could see the metal returning. As the model vanished, she returned the gear to its place and then pushed open the door.

A pair of guards shouted in alarm and began shooting her armor with handguns, so she quickly shot both of them right back. "Room clear!" she shouted into the radio.

A bank of security monitors and a computer, very similar to the one she'd found in the HQ building occupied the room. She quickly stripped one gauntlet and tried to log into the computer, but it rejected her. She guessed they'd finally gotten around to locking her out.

Instead, she grabbed one of the guards' hands and pressed it to the reader, holding her breath. The light turned green and the terminal displayed a welcome message. She dropped the dead guard's arm and began digging.

It took almost no time to find the control to unlock the doors, but she wasn't ready yet. She dug through the records, looking for the room Sasha was in, but found nothing. Growing impatient, she went through the security feeds, focusing on the holding cells.

In a few minutes, she began to curse vehemently. She only realized she was transmitting when Legolas said over the radio, "Amanda, what's wrong?"

"The holding cells are empty. All of them. I'm in the computer in the control room, and there's no-one here. Fuck! I have no idea where else she would be! The orders I forged were to bring her here and put her in a holding cell."

"Okay, calm down," David joined in, "Where else would they have put her, given who she is?"

Amanda thought. "Maybe the tech lab? There's supposed to be one here, down on the tenth floor…"

"Alright, down to the tenth we go, then." Gimli sounded unfazed by this new development. Amanda walked out of the control room and found herself in the lead this time, with Gimli in the rear. He gestured for her to lead the way, so she did.

They returned to the stairs and went down four flights to the tenth floor. Once again, they stacked up on the door and breached. Amanda performed the maneuver instinctively, the motions and timing being fed to her brain and legs by Flytrap.

This door opened to a corridor. Windows on the side opened onto rooms full of electrical, mechanical and computer gear. Tool boxes hung from the walls next to first aid kits and fire extinguishers.

They made their way more slowly than Amanda would have liked. Gimli opined that, while the enemies weapons were ineffective against their armor, there was plenty of stuff around here that could be weaponized, so they traded off a bit of their haste for caution, peeking into rooms that didn't have windows and moving with a deliberate pace. Amanda began noting the location of cutting lasers and large rivet guns in the rooms, finding a fair number of them.

She made contact after her third turn, when a bullet struck her armor with a heavy thwack and sent her flipping onto her back. Red indicators lit up, then faded to yellow and then green as she struggled to catch her breath, shooting blinding in the direction the round had come from.

She finally sucked in some air as she climbed back to her feet. The others had stopped shooting along with her, so she stopped as well, checking her ammo counter and finding it in the single digits. She swapped magazines without looking, the tactile sensors in her armor making it easy.

At the end of this branch, a man in black tactical gear lay bleeding on the floor. Amanda walked forward, and without exposing herself to the turn at the end, seized the man by one foot and dragged him back. He still clutched a gun in his hands.

"What the hell kind of gun is that?" Amanda asked. "It hurt."

Gimli glanced down. "Carbine version of an anti-material semi-auto sniper rifle. Huge fucking bullet, lots of fuel packed in the case. This guy's dressed differently, any idea why?"

"He's Black Team," Amanda said, recognizing his gear from photos she'd seen on the computers at the Viridian headquarters building.

"Viridian security Spec-Ops. Not as secretive as DevSec, but plenty dangerous. Recruited from Tier One units in the military. They shouldn't be here unless…"

She trailed off, the realization sinking in. Black Team operations were almost all done under the auspices of DevSec. She didn't know what they did because she'd been denied access to the reports, but she'd found a list of Black Team operations and the divisions they'd done them on behalf of.

"I think DevSec might be here," she said.

"What's that?" Gimli asked.

"The division I was a part of. It's Viridian's highest-tier security force. There's a Draughtgen woman leading it up, and I'm pretty sure any Operators she brought will be in power armor, like us."

"Well, that's not ideal," David said.

Gimli laughed again. "Y'all just stay behind Legolas and me. We'll handle it," he said. He continued, addressing Legolas, "You scared of a couple of 'Tier One' mercs, Legolas?"

"I think we'll be fine," Legolas said mildly. Since they seemed so sure of themselves, Amanda let the two of them get in front, and they quickly rushed around the corner. No shots fired, and she moved forward, David on her rear.

This hall had only a single door at the far end. They moved forward and Gimli didn't bother stacking up on it, kicking it open as soon as he got there and rushing in. Amanda heard more of the loud reports from the Black Team rifles, along with the clack-crack of the pair's assault rifles. By the time she'd followed them in, it was over.

Three black-clad mercenaries lay on the floor. Gimli and Legolas kicked their rifles away from them. The room seemed to be a staging room, with lockers lining the walls and safety signs scattered around. A glass door on the far end showed what looked like a decontamination room; vents in the walls and ceilings through which gasses could be pumped to disinfect anyone inside.

Legolas was closer once they got all the enemy weapons strewn into a corner, so he walked up to the glass door and hit a large red button. The doors opened, and he raised his rifle and sprayed automatic fire, shattering the far door.

He reloaded smoothly as he stepped through. Amanda got right behind him and walked through the decon room.

Sasha was laying on a surgical table. The table was angled to keep her in a sitting position, and the back of her head was opened the same way Amanda's had been in the video she'd seen of Mike's death. Amanda rushed forward and checked.

There were components missing from Sasha's head. A monitor just to the side of the bed beeped steadily with biological readings. She glanced over it and saw that it was showing a steady heartbeat and healthy temperature. David came up behind her and turned the monitor.

"She's alive," he said, "Sedated. I have no idea why they opened her up. Amanda?"

Amanda looked over the inside. A couple of wires were free, dangling loosely. She could see connectors on some of the parts that had nothing plugged into them.

"They were taking her apart," she said. "I think they were accessing her memories, but…"

She looked around. There were components on a side table, ready to be put in but she knew they weren't the missing ones. They were the wrong shapes. She examined them for a moment before she realized what she was looking at.

"These are Seven series components. They didn't come out of Sasha's head."

"So they were putting these in?" David asked.

"I guess… I don't know-" Amanda stopped. "Wait…. I think they already got what they wanted as far as the drive is concerned. The modules they removed, they're the same ones that were damaged in my head when I was shot. I think they're experimenting now, putting these in, maybe trying to figure out what happened to me? Maybe trying to see if they could make an effective military model with cheaper components? I'm not sure."

"What would they have done with the parts they pulled out?" Gimli asked. Legolas answered for him. "Here," he said, and pointed to a side table. Gimli looked over and shook his head.

"I don't think we're gonna be putting these back together, so, how much of this other crap do we have to bring with us to leave with her in this state?" Gimli asked.

David answered, "The bio stuff is just monitoring equipment and a dose regulator for the sedative. We can unhook her and, biologically at least, she'll be fine."

"Okay then, we already know she'll survive having these other components put in, because you're running around with them in your head, now. So scoop 'em up, scoop her up and let's go. Cindy can put them in her head when we get back."

Amanda gathered up the components on the tray while David unhooked Sasha. He placed his hand over her chest and asked Amanda "Ten thousand volts, right?"

"What?" she asked.

"To close her head up."

"I don't know. Mike used a taser, I don't know what the voltage on those are."

David turned his head towards Legolas, next to him.

"Mainline human tasers are usually eight to twelve thousand volts. Ten thousand is right in the middle, so…"

The implication was clear. They weren't sure, but didn't have a way to confirm. With a sigh, David hooked Sasha back up to the monitoring equipment. "There's resuscitation gear built in, in case something goes wrong," he explained.

He put his hand on her chest again, and Sasha jerked. Her head closed.

"Ten thousand volts," David said.

He unhooked her and scooped her up again. "Ready," he announced.

"Okay, David's hands are full, so Amanda, you're gonna have to cover him. Me and Legolas will punch the hole."

They moved out. They made it to the stairwell and began heading down, but ran into a problem. Just below the sixth floor, a dense foam had filled the stairwell, cutting off their route back down. Gimli prodded it with his gun barrel, but it was stiff and unyielding.

"Well, looks like backup has arrived. Or else the rest of the guards on site have gotten organized. Amanda, what's on the sixth floor?"

"Another open office, like the twelfth, but with server rooms and an IT department where the holding cells were."

She saw Gimli's shoulders shrug. "Well, our route out is blocked, and there's a big, open space left clear for us to enter. That doesn't sound at all like a trap." Sarcasm notwithstanding, he stacked up on the door to the sixth floor.

"This is probably going to be a big fight. Legolas, if you think raging will help, you go right ahead, and I'll cover you. If not, hang back, punch through the drop ceiling and use thermals to cover the rest of us. Amanda, the two of us are going in hard and fast. David, drop her here, get your gun up and wait till it's clear to move forward. Reload if you're not topped off, including your underbarrel. We've got the target with us, so collateral damage isn't much of an issue right now. Odds are, there's a shit-ton of 'em on the other side of this door, just waiting for us."

"That's your plan," Amanda asked incredulously, "To just rush in hard?"

"Well, I wasn't quite done yet," Glmli scolded, his tone patronizing. "What you and are are going to do is to blaze a trail to the right of this door, straight to the exterior wall. I'll drop a demo charge on it to make a big hole, and then we get out through that. I'll slave your thrusters again, so just jump out and try not to wiggle too much when it's your turn. David will get Sasha. Cindy's lining up now.

"We'll get to the van, get the fuck out of here, and we'll fix Sasha up back at the apartment. Everybody cool?"

David and Legolas agreed. Amanda muttered something affirmative into the radio, but the bad feeling she'd been nursing this whole time was all but shouting at her now. They were doing exactly what the enemy wanted. If the damned stairwell weren't so small, she'd demand Gimli use his charge there. But the blast would probably kill them all, armor or not.

Gimli counted down again. On zero, he burst through the door and all hell broke loose.

Avenged

Wednesday, December 30th, 2759

Amanda rushed into the maelstrom after Gimli. Bullets immediately began ricocheting off her armor as she followed him to the right. She fired back on full auto, simply spraying and praying.

Her prayers were answered in the worst possible way. There had to be over a hundred Viridian Security mercenaries in the vast room, and she could pretty much close her eyes and fire, and still hit someone. They crowded her and Gimli's route, and she had to swing her barrel back and forth between shooting at the huge mass of them to her left and shooting those in front of her whom Gimli hadn't killed yet.

She swung her barrel back to the left and triggered three grenades, spreading them out. Before they even landed, explosions rocked the floor from Gimli's own use of his underbarrel.

As the explosions of her grenades filled the room even more with dust and debris, she saw the far wall rush up to meet her. She stopped and turned, facing back to cover Gimli while he set up the charge. She knew they'd have to rush back before it exploded, and she wanted to keep the route clear.

She fired until her magazine ran dry, then reloaded. There was no sign of Legolas other than a large hole in the drop ceiling just in front of the stairwell door, and the puffs of material that came out of the ceiling, moving slightly differently than the puffs from stray rounds hitting it. Each such puff resulted in an enemy falling over out of sight, probably dead. They seemed unaware of Legolas, but it wouldn't be long before they figured out there was someone up above the tiles, shooting them.

Gimli finished his work and called out "Cover!"

Amanda and Gimli rushed back the way they'd come. Legolas fell out of the ceiling to join them and they got inside the stairwell.

"Fire in the fuckin' hole!" Gimli shouted and the whole world shook.

Amanda was still moving when he called it. She was thrown towards, and then over the stairwell. She landed a flight down with a heavy metallic clatter and a sharp exhalation. For the second time in ten minutes, she struggles to suck in air. She got her feet underneath her and moved quickly up the stairs, her vision growing dim at the edges from the lack of oxygen, until with a blessed relief, she managed to inhale fully.

The others were already moving towards the hole in the side of the building. Most of her vision consisted of smoke and dust, and the armor had to overlay glowing yellow lines onto everything, in order for her to see enough to proceed. Legolas jumped out first, thrusters on his back and legs firing immediately as he dropped out of sight a hair slower than he would have without them.

David followed, carrying Sasha. Amanda felt a flood of relief wash over her as he leaped out and his own thrusters fired. Gimli went next. As he leaped, he spun. His thrusters fired large plumes of exhaust from the others, and he hovered in place, firing his rifle over Amanda's head and around her. Every few shots, he fired the grenade launcher as well, and Amanda felt the explosions behind her, propelling her forward.

She reached the opening and right as she leaped, she heard the loud report of one of Black Team's rifles, right as a sledgehammer struck her left arm and spun her around. At the same instant, her thrusters fired… Propelling her right back into the building.

Amanda cursed as she flew back in, through the worst of the dust and smoke. She clattered to the floor, rolling to absorb the impact and get her feet under her.

"Shit!" she heard Gimli say, "Amanda's still in, I'm going-" he cut off abruptly as another explosion shook the building.

He spoke again a second later, "They've got air cover! Get to the deck and get lost, I've got Amanda!"

She opened her mouth to speak, but no words came. A figure stepped into view in front of her. The figure wore power armor that was noticeably different from the armor Amanda wore. It had a clear faceplate, and Amanda recognized the face there.

Rachel Hornsby.

"I've been hoping to run into you," Rachel said. Amanda clocked her hands, but saw no weapons there. "I don't appreciate my property betraying me like that."

"I'm not your property," Amanda shot back, flipping on her external speakers. She began to raise her rifle, then realized with a start she wasn't carrying it. She must have lost it when her thrusters misfired.

"Oh yes you are, Aster. Arthesian law doesn't have any provision for sentient machines." Rachel darted forward, swinging an armored fist at Amanda's face.

Amanda slapped the blow aside and body-checked Rachel with her shoulder.

"The word is sapient, you dumb cunt," she muttered, swinging a fist of her own at the back of Rachel's head. Rachel was too fast however, and dodged it, spinning and kicking Amanda's legs out from under her. Amanda fell backwards onto the floor, Rachel swarming her before she even landed.

Blows rained down on her. They hurt, as armored gauntlets impacted her helmet and the sensations were duly transmitted through. They didn't hurt as much as they should, but they still hurt. Amanda got her own arms up to protect her head as the indicators began to turn yellow on her HUD, only to have Rachel straighten and stomp down on her chest. For the third time, the air rushed out of her lungs. Amanda squeaked out a breathless growl and raised her own leg, snapping her heel into Rachel's crotch and shoving her back.

Amanda rolled to her feet right as Rachel rushed her, and quickly ducked back down, wrapping her arms around the other woman's waist. She straightened and fell over backwards, gripping tightly. The same move she'd used on Sasha. The clatter as their armor struck the concrete floor was deafening. Amanda spun on her butt as Rachel's legs wrapped around her waist in turn. She landed a solid punch into Rachel's faceplate, and saw the transparent material crack under her fist. But then Rachel arched her back, and Amanda couldn't reach her head any more. Instead, Amanda slammed both fists down into Rachel's crotch, eliciting a cry of pain. She grimaced savagely and did it again. Rachel cried out again, louder.

Rachel spun, knocking Amanda off her own knees and then curled back up. She threw a flurry of blows at Amanda, knocking her helmet back and forth as she tried to get her feet back underneath her. But Rachel still had her legs clamped around Amanda's waist, and the weight dragged at her.

She focused on the movement assist icon, and it opened up to display that movement assist was currently at 60%. She ramped it up to 100 and thrashed.

The motion flung her off the ground and out of Rachel's grip, tumbling and rolling away. She got her legs underneath her just in time to see Rachel lifting one of the Black Team rifles. Amanda rushed forwards, but she was not fast enough.

The first round knocked her backwards off her feet again. The next set off loud warning tones and pushed her backwards. The third turned half of her status indicators red.

Amanda slapped her arms out and felt something. She pulled it to her as she rolled sideways and realized that it was her rifle. A fourth and fifth shot struck the floor where she'd just been. As soon as she grabbed it, the weapons interface reappeared. She clicked the ammo mode over from Frangible to Armor Piercing and raised it right as the sixth round from Rachel's gun struck her hip.

Pain exploded through her torso, but she gritted her teeth and got the glowing crosshairs lined up on the silhouette before her. She squeezed the trigger and felt a grim satisfaction as Rachel cried out again and reeled backwards.

Amanda rose, firing the underbarrel now that Rachel was a bit further away. The proximity still rocked her when the grenade went off, but she moved forward through the shockwave, grimly determined to end this.

Rachel rolled out of view behind a pile of rubble mixed with bodies. Amanda quickly fired a grenade at the other side of the pile and rushed around behind her.

Rachel had gotten her feet in that split second. The explosion might have staggered her, but hadn't knocked her down. She fired again, and the round hit Amanda in the chest.

It hurt. It hurt a lot. Status indicators went red all over her armor, and her chestplate went black. The medical system flashed the letters GSW - Chest in front of her as it went into overdrive, pumping her with drugs and nanites.

Amanda knew her armor couldn't take much more. The indicator told her that she had multiple broken ribs, and she felt the sudden warm rush of the painkillers being injected by the armor. A buzzing tension followed as the armor, knowing she was still fighting, followed that up with stimulants to keep from compromising her too much.

She fired her main barrel again, aiming at Rachel's faceplate. The rounds impacted with crunching smacks, and Amanda saw splinters flying. She held the trigger down until the magazine ran dry, knocking the woman right back off her feet.

Another shot from Rachel struck her, and this one felt different. Weakness immediately spread from her stomach where it had impacted, and she felt loose and disconnected. The medical status changed and now read `2X GSW - Chest, Gut`. She ignored it and strode forward as the pain from her gut began to grow. Rachel's rifle clicked. Empty.

Rachel's faceplate was almost gone, but the face under it was merely abraded and bruised. Her eyes were active, watching Amanda as she kicked the weapon out of her hands.

"Truth be told, I don't even remember you," Amanda said as she dropped both knees on Rachel's chest, driving the air of her lungs with a sharp 'oof!'

"But I bet I fucking hated you," she finished. She drove a fist down into the remains of Rachel's faceplate and felt it shatter and release. With the movement assist dialed up, her fist continued through the ruined armor, through the face beneath, through the skull and brain behind that, and clanged off of the back of Rachel's helmet.

Amanda straightened, gore dripping from her left hand. She felt another hand come down on her shoulder and heard Gimli's voice.

"Come on! We've got to move!"

She stood, the pain from her gut almost disabling now, and swayed on her feet. "Oh, shit," Gimli said when he saw her. "No, lay the fuck back down, gods damnit…"

Amanda complied. It was easy, because her knees buckled from the pain. She collapsed onto her side, then rolled onto her back. She heard a quiet mewling sound, and was startled to realize it was her. She clamped her teeth down and tried to remain quiet.

Gimli retrieved a case from his storage compartment and opened it. A small bot crawled out, ran over to her belly and crouched there on six spider-like legs. Amanda lifted her head and saw blood covering her torso and running down her legs.

"You've been gut-shot," Gimli told her, "And by one of those big guns, from the looks of it. Let the bot stitch you up."

Small tools extended from the bot's underside and began working on her. It was excruciating at first, and she cried out involuntarily, but after a few seconds, a numbness began to spread. The ripping, burning sensations of the bot working turned into muted tugs that reminded her of Sasha digging the bullet out of her back.

The bot worked quickly. A minute and a half after it had first started, it drew all the tools back into its body and returned to the case. Gimli stowed it and held out a hand to Amanda.

She took it and he pulled her to her feet. The weakness was still there, but the pain was a hollow echo of what it had been. "No time to patch your armor up. Your thrusters look good. Well, good-ish, so let's go."

He led her back to the hole in the side of the building and stuck his head out experimentally. Amanda realized he'd stowed his rifle on his back and was carrying one of the Black Team guns. A couple of magazines for it were stuck to his leg, held in place by what she assumed were magnets.

After looking around, he nodded. "Looks clear, but they have armed fliers in the air, so we're going to have to drop out, and trigger thrusters to cushion our landing. The van's gone, so we're gonna hoof it a couple of blocks, until we can rendezvous with the others. You good to go?"

"Do I have a choice?" Amanda asked. She could hear the grin as he replied, "Nope."

Gimli went first, stepping out and dropping like a stone. Amand held her breath as she did the same, her stomach rising into her throat as she fell.

Both of their thrusters fired at the same instant. Gimli slammed into the ground hard, crouching to absorb the energy. Amanda hit less hard, having been higher than him, but her knees still buckled and she collapsed, a fresh pain erupting in her gut, powering through the painkillers. She scrambled to her feet quickly as Gimli peered around over the barrel of his stolen rifle.

"One's coming," he said into the radio. "Use your grenade launcher."

Amanda hauled her legs up underneath her, then gave up on standing for the moment. She raised her rifle and pointed it at the sky where Gimli was focused.

A distant whine grew louder, and then a shadow appeared above them. Gimli gave it a second to emerge fully from behind the roof of a nearby building, then fired once. Amanda saw one of the engines immediately begin to spit sparks and a thick cloud of black smoke. The sound of the engines grew louder and higher pitched. She put her crosshairs on the flier's belly and squeezed the trigger. The grenade launcher ejected the shell, which arced up and then exploded as it struck the flier.

The flier's engines screamed as it dropped like a stone. It struck the pavement a hundred meters south of them with a horrible crunch that set off nearby car alarms.

"Let's move. North two blocks, then West three." He took off. Amanda pushed herself to her feet and jogged to catch up with him.

They encountered no resistance on the streets. The ever-present crowds gave them a wide berth, exclaiming at their appearance and armaments. A few people screamed when they saw them, but most simply moved away, talking excitedly to each other and raising their phones to take video.

They moved the two blocks north, then hung a left on a narrower road. The crowds were thinner, so Gimli picked up the pace. Amanda strained to match him, nausea and agony growing as she moved.

They made the three blocks in the same time it had taken them to make the previous two. Gimli stopped at the corner and waited for Amanda.

"Van's on the way," he said simply as Amanda bellowed deep breaths and tried not to vomit in her suit. The pain in her gut was getting worse, and it sent chills through her.

Before she could catch her breath, the van came around a corner, and Amanda could see Cindy behind the wheel. She felt relief wash over her as it quickly screeched to a stop and the side doors opened. Legolas and David were in the back, helmets off, Sasha laying insensate across their laps. Amanda climbed in, Gimli hot on her heels and the door closed on its own.

Tires squealed, the percussive drive clattered and they were off.

Daisy

Accomplished

Cindy pulled up to the resident's entrance and insisted they all get out of their armor before disembarking the van. David grabbed a duffel bag and held it open while Amanda dumped the components in. Gimli grabbed another bag and retrieved towels from it which he passed out. Legolas and David got Sasha out, laid her down on the carpet in front of the door and accepted towels. They wiped off the gel that covered their bodies and got dressed in the clothes Gimli dug out next. Amanda picked Sasha up and cradled her. She declined the offer of sweatpants and a t-shirt, not wanting to let Sasha go. Her weight was comforting, even as it strained her injured torso.

Cindy pulled away without explaining where she was going. The others didn't question her, and Amanda was too tired to. They walked in and headed for the elevators. Tourists gawked at them, mafioso in expensive suits studiously ignored them, and tattooed gangsters smirked. Amanda reflected that this might not even be the first time they'd seen a naked, wounded woman carrying a naked, unconscious woman through the lobby.

They rode up to the top floor and walked in. Amanda deposited Sasha in a bedroom David showed her, and then collapsed on the bed next to her. She slipped into a dreamless sleep within seconds.

When she awoke a few hours later, Cindy was back. She'd brought tools and gear to work on Sasha. Amanda started to get up, but David came in with a large bag with "Medical" written on the side. "No," he said, "Stay in bed. Lay on your back. You've still got a through-and-through in your chest and I need to check the bot's work on your stomach."

Amanda didn't know if one or both of them were experts in this, or if they simply had such advanced gear, but they worked quickly. Cindy installed the components they'd brought with them while David sicced another spider-like bot on her chest wound and examined her stomach wound. He ran a tissue regenerator over both, a more advanced model that made both wound itch and tingle intensely. When he was done, the redness was mostly gone.

"I scanned your head while you were unconscious," Cindy said. "To get an idea of what was going on with you. You were right; these components and the ones in your head are a match. It really looks like they planned to do the same thing to her that was done to you."

"So what does that mean, for her?" Amanda asked. Cindy shrugged. "I don't know. The tech isn't something I'm familiar with. I could do a lot more scans and maybe make some educated guesses, but honestly, the fastest way to find out is to wait for her to wake up."

Amanda nodded. Apprehension grew, but there was nothing she could do but wait.

She dozed back off in the chair and woke up to Gimli shaking her. "Sasha's starting to come around. Figured you'd want to be here for this." Legolas stood on the other side of the bed.

Amanda stood, walking to the side of the bed. Gimli stood beside her. She wished the two of them would leave, but she understood that they didn't know what to expect. Neither one appeared to be armed, and if Sasha was violent, she'd appreciate the help subduing her.

Sasha stirred, shaking her head back and forth. After a few minutes, she opened her eyes and they focused on Amanda.

"A… Amanda?" she asked. "Yeah, it's me," Amanda responded, trepidation filling her. Sasha's memory seemed to be intact. Amanda wondered if Sasha would attack her again.

"What… What happened."

"You were hurt," Amanda said, "We patched you back up."

Amanda sat on the side of the bed and Sasha reached out for her hand. "Who are these two?" she asked, eyes flicking back and forth between Legolas and Gimli.

"The short guy is Gimli, the taller one is Legolas," Amanda said. Sasha grinned sleepily. "I love the Lord of the Rings," she said.

"What's the last thing you remember?" Amanda asked her.

"Umm," Sasha said, frowning. "We were going to look for that guy you told me about. Ming, I think. We had just left the jewelers."

Amanda nodded. "What's the first thing you remember? Like, ever?"

Sasha's frown deepened and she sat up. "Wait…" she said, holding up a finger and turning her head from side to side as if the answer might tumble free.

"I… Oh my god, I can't…"

"It's amnesia, Sasha." The relief Amanda felt warred with guilt. "We knew this might happen. I found out what caused mine, and then the same thing happened to you. Just please, try to recall your oldest memories."

"I remember meeting you… Oh my god…. There's nothing else, I can't remember anything else!"

Amanda wrapped her arms around her and held her tight as she sobbed.

They had called for a ship to transport them off planet, but it would take several days to arrive. During that time, Amanda filled in the gaps in Sasha's memory as best as she could. She explained the component swap that had caused their memory loss. She explained Sasha's violent break, their capture, and the rescue.

Sasha's memory loss worked differently than Amanda's, which was both a blessing and a curse. The personality she had adopted in her role to track down Amanda had seemingly become permanent. An unexpected side effect had been that, through some strange trick of digital psychology, the new personality had helped preserve some of her more recent memories.The ones she had formed while wearing this new personality.

With Cindy's help, they discovered memory banks in the behavioral module. Memory banks that were used to store cover personalities and useful memories. In Sasha's case, she had most of her memories since their meeting at the store: any time she was acting in her role as the excitable, socially awkward medical student. Amanda wondered if the same thing might have happened to her. She wondered if the original Amanda felt the same way she did, or if her personality was just some sort of cover that had become permanent.

It provided an answer as to why she'd remembered Mike and David's names. David was an operationally important detail. She had known that he would be the one heading out, since Cindy had been involved in the op to pull the evidence, an op which had gone bad, injured or killed everyone involved and possibly blown her cover. As for Mike, Amanda could only conclude that she'd purposefully shifted memory of him over to this storage. A sort of memorial, able to survive the amnesia she knew was coming.

Either way, the effect it had on Sasha was clear. This Sasha was the one that Amanda had met in the cosmetic store days ago, not the operative that had tracked her and attacked her outside of the secured site. What once was a lie had become the truth. Sasha had trouble accepting that she wasn't really a medical student who worked at a cosmetics shop, but she worked gamely to do so.

As far as Amanda was concerned, the lie was better than the original truth. The original Sasha had, rather than trusting Amanda, decided that she intended to abandon her. Amanda didn't know how that had happened, but she knew from what Cindy and David told her that it wasn't true. Amanda had always planned to bring Sasha with her. Whatever she'd done to undermine the original Sasha's faith in her was unknown. But this new Sasha trusted her again. Amanda vowed grimly to herself that she would not give her another reason not to.

Sasha was mortified to learn the truth of who she had been, and how she'd attacked Amanda outside the secured site. She broke down and cried several times. Amanda held her and reminded her that it wasn't her who had done those things.

This new Sasha didn't know she had a BCI, so it took some time for her to access it. When she finally did, she discovered that it had the same software as Amandas, complete with links to the behavioral module. She swore she'd never use Flytrap, and Amanda prayed that she wouldn't ever have to, either. Sasha tried to access memories earlier than the cosmetic store, but using Cindy's equipment to monitor her hardware as she did so, it quickly became apparent that those memories simply weren't there.

And there was bad news, too. The software they were running was far too much for the hardware in their heads. They had yet to experience any symptoms, but it would be just a few more weeks before it happened. Memory loss, emotional outbursts, chaotic shifts in active State codes… Both Amanda and Sasha were teetering on the edge of a psychotic break, and if they didn't do something soon, it would be the death of both of them.

Cindy stepped up, going out of her way to help. She raided several of their secured sites (the one in the forest had been but one of many) and retrieved unused equipment. She managed to jerry rig some of the more advanced Imperial systems into new components for both of them. It wasn't a permanent fix, but it would tide them over long enough to get to Imperial space.

Amanda played with her state codes. Flipping them on and off, exploring them, figuring out what they were best at. Flytrap was obvious. Orchid helped her think tactically and deal with subterfuge and spycraft. Rose contained instincts for acting and playing a role, and a whole lot of instinctive understanding of human psychology.

The final one, Chamomile, had a host of warnings whenever she examined it, and an ominous, single word description. Contagion. Everyone agreed not to try that one until they could get some computer experts to examine the code. Whatever it did, it wasn't good, but it was a mystery for another day.

She still had plenty of those. Her memories of being abused. Why she looked like a Seven series, while Sasha didn't resemble any of the Viridian sex-bots. How, exactly, their retrieval of the drive had gone wrong. What her exact role in Viridian had been. Why they had been built in the first place. If the

Amanda she was now was the same Amanda she had been, before.

True to her word, Cindy showed Amanda the rest of the interview. Amanda watched it with Sasha, and together, they learned more about their pasts. At the heart of the matter was the clonal tissue construction tech that Viridian touted so much. Viridian had spent billions trying to develop it, and billions more trying to cover up the fact that they'd never succeeded. The tech didn't exist.

Instead, Viridian was cloning full human bodies, using tissue regenerators to accelerate their growth through childhood and puberty, and then lobotomizing them to make room for the components when they reached adulthood. They had stopped all research into the clonal tissue construction as well, because the cost of running tissue regenerators was cheaper than the expected cost of constructing tiny-brained bodies from cloned tissue.

They were killing children wholesale to harvest their bodies, and making hundreds of billions in profit as a result. The whole scheme had been the brainchild of Rachel Hornsby, head of DevSec.

Their efforts to recruit Draughtgen for their security divisions was a cover for their real goal: to find an isolated location, far from any prying eyes, where they could expand their operation. They found a planet slated for colonization in Imperial space, and worked out a deal with the Office of Colonization to purchase the colony rights. Regular inspections were a part of that deal, but they had set up a real colony, along with several factories as a cover story. The actual expansion site was to be built underground, on the opposite side of the planet.

Rachel Hornsby had been recruited not because she was a veteran, but because of her expertise in genetics. She had been the one to design and grow the first clone. The whole Seven series project was her darling.

Amanda and Sasha had been an offshoot of that. Rachel had understood the military potential, and modified her designs to have Draughtgen physiology. Six clones had been grown, murdered and had computers stuffed into their heads.

The project had been a very limited success. The resulting bots had much more advanced hardware and software, and full sapience had been inevitable and even planned for. After two years, four of the six had experienced catastrophic emotional breakdowns and been terminated. Only Amanda and Sasha had survived. They had been assigned to lead Black Team units, and had been involved in several illegal activities over the decade of their existence.

Until one day, Amanda had been doing research in Viridian's libraries for some mission on New Canada when she stumbled across sealed records. Curiosity got the better of her, and she forced her way in.

She'd been horrified to learn of the truth. Tens of thousands of young girls, forced to grow up over the span of a few years and then murdered, to make a product that was designed to be abused.

She'd gone straight to the Imperial Embassy, knowing that the massive nation would have both the resources and motivations to help her. That's where she met Cindy. They had made a deal, and then Amanda had returned after completing her mission.

Cindy and David had followed, bringing Gimli and Legolas to run security. They had carefully planned an operation to get the proof they needed to send Imperial law enforcement after the foreign company, using their operations in Imperial space to establish jurisdiction.

Amanda had used Viridian's local recruiting efforts to draw in some street toughs, whom she could entice with no-limit expense accounts and six-digit salaries to help her. Most of the people this had produced were too sketchy for her to trust, but one of them had managed to impress her with his integrity. Mike.

Despite looking and acting the part, just like the others, Mike had a sense of honor that would shine through from time to time. She had observed him for weeks before approaching him, and decided that, as long as she earned his trust, he could be trusted in turn.

So she'd honeypotted him. She approached him, not appealing to his conscience at first, but to his libido. She presented herself as a high ranking security operative (which was true) who enjoyed slumming it with street kids, something for which she already had a reputation (though it was not exactly true). She took Mike out and spent a night with him, and as she'd suspected, he called her back the next day to do it again. Despite his swaggering bravado, and brash mannerisms, he had remained respectful and considerate. When he asked her for a second date, he'd grinned like he knew she would never say no, and left her an easy out, anyways. Of course, she said yes, she had plans for him. But she couldn't help but be charmed by the odd mix of confidence and conscience.

Her plan had been relatively straightforward. Mike provided a cover, which she could use to meet with Cindy to develop their plans. Mike was also a resource; a skilled fighter who could help her when it came time to steal the evidence. And, very quickly, she'd come to genuinely enjoy their time together. She had eventually told him the truth, and he agreed without hesitation to help her.

Amanda watched her face carefully as she spoke of Mike, and she could see it. She'd loved him. Obviously not at first, but in time, as she got to know him. She watched as she spoke of him in the interview, and saw the tenderness in her own eyes as she described him. The relief was palpable.

Amanda watched Sasha as this part played out. She didn't know how she'd done it, but she had. She'd been in love with two completely different people. This seemed to provide an answer to Amanda's questions about her personality. Amanda couldn't comprehend maintaining two relationships like that. But at one point, she could.

For all of her affections for Mike, she still saw herself describe Sasha as the most reliable, trustworthy person she'd ever known. Her best friend, her secret lover. She looked over at the woman sitting next to her, watching the interview with her, and listened to her own voice talk about the time they'd spent together.

Early on in their lives, Viridian had prohibited Amanda and Sasha from developing a personal relationship. Two of the others had done so, and that had precipitated the emotional break they'd suffered. The company had quartered them on opposite sides of the security bunker, and though they were permitted wide latitude to operate on their own, they were watched like a hawk in their downtime.

Amanda's trick of using Mike as cover was one she'd used before, to meet with Sasha. She would pick up some horny kid who was enraptured by her well-designed charms, string him along and have him take her out. They'd have enough of a good time to keep him from getting suspicious, and then she would insist upon seeing herself home, at which point she could meet in secret with Sasha. They had never met at the same place twice, and their meetings usually consisted of little more than a quick meal and an overnight stay in a hotel. But it had been those secret trysts for which Amanda lived. It was those nights that made the rest of her existence worthwhile.

The recorded Amanda didn't say how her and Sasha had started seeing each other, which filled the present Amanda with disappointment. But in the end, it didn't matter. Sasha took her hand as the recording talked of how much Sasha had meant to her. They watched, feeling the predictable, yet inescapable tension as Amanda described how Sasha had grown cold.

Sasha knew about Mlke, of course. And she knew about Amanda's trick of using men as an excuse to get out to see her, of course, because she did the same herself. She didn't understand, however, why Amanda had started calling off their trysts.

The recorded Amanda wasn't sure, but she suspected that Sasha had been following her. She thought Sasha might know that something else was going on, as Amanda quietly left Mike's home in the dark of the night and vanished into the city. Amanda had planned to tell her.

The interview had happened before the raid to collect the evidence. Cindy didn't know if Amanda had spoken to Sasha or not before that, and Amanda, of course, couldn't remember. They didn't know what went wrong, but it was clear that something had.

The interview was a little over an hour long, and by the end of it, Amanda's eyes were wet with tears. She wept for Mike, who'd sacrificed himself so valiantly in the name of a cause he knew he'd been manipulated into. He hadn't cared one bit that Amanda had used him at first. He had loved her, and he had believed they were doing the right thing.

She wept for the lost memories with Sasha and Mike, memories that were so important, but were now gone, never to be recovered. She wept for the tens of thousands of girls who'd been brutally murdered, so that their bodies could be turned into playthings for lonely men.

At the end, both she and Sasha were exhausted. They'd slept for hours in the bedroom, and then locked the door and made passionate love. They stayed in the room together, talking quietly or exploring each other, learning again what had once been so important to each of them.

Their ship arrived, and the six of them drove to the spaceport. They boarded the orbiter and launched, docking with the ship after the short flight into orbit. Onboard, Amanda found a viewport with a clear view of the planet below.

From up here, it was beautiful. The throngs of stressed out, overworked and underpaid people, the piles of garbage, the crime, the flaunted excess… None of it could be seen. Only great green swathes of continent, broken by brown and white mountains and speckled with gray cities, surrounded by the glittering blue oceans and swathed in a blanket of white clouds.

Amanda watched the planet shrink as they moved off, and then watched it distort and twist as they entered warp. Whatever the future held for her, she was determined never to return.

Epilogue: Assigned

Friday, June 12th, 2781

As the orbital shuttle descended through the roiling chaos of a thunderstorm, Amanda closed the mission files she'd been reviewing and brought up her own files. Even now, more than a year later, she was still reeling from the violence of her earliest memories.

Upon her and Sasha's arrival at the Imperial Embassy on New Canada, they had been offered places in the Imperial Central Intelligence Bureau by Cindy and Dave's boss, a large, genial man who went by Bruce and made a point of running the embassy kitchens for the breakfast shift, every morning.

Bruce had made it clear that they were free to refuse, and to simply disappear with the eight-digit bank accounts they were owed, as per their original agreement. But he stressed the importance of the work they were doing, pointing to the peaceful, prosperous world on which they stood and explaining its history. Destroyed, with the vast majority of the population wiped out by a combination of an alien invasion and a reanimation pandemic, the local ICIB presence had shifted from covert to overt operations, establishing an embassy and helping the few survivors rebuild their world. They had used their sway to draw in elements of the Imperial Defense Force, the largest military in the galaxy, bringing skilled engineers and logistics experts in to make sure the rebuilding happened with the IDF's characteristic, brutal efficiency.

Bruce also made it clear that the repairs they both needed so badly would be funded and performed by the ICIB. They would get the best components in the galaxy, installed by the best technicians in the galaxy, if they joined. If they didn't, they would be responsible for finding the parts and technicians themselves. He assured them that it could be done, and without too much difficulty. But the price would be high, immediately taking a big chunk out of their funds.

And the truth was, neither Sasha nor Amanda knew what to do with themselves, now. Their plans, even before their mutual memory losses, had never extended beyond this part. When Bruce let them both believe that the offer was to stay there and help continue the rebuilding efforts -which would last another ten years or more- they agreed readily.

And once it had its grips on them, the ICIB did what any self-respecting intelligence apparatus would; whatever the hell it wanted.

Thus it was that Amanda and Sasha had undergone another band-aid fix; just enough to tide them over through their training, and then spent eleven months running an intensive field-agent course, along with a dozen other graduates of the ICIB's universal basic training. They had excelled, of course. Unlike the others, they were both literally built for this work, and they had stood head and shoulders above their classmates. Switching and even blending State codes had become second nature to them both over the course of this training, and as if to punish them for doing too well, they'd been given different assignments at the end.

They had a scant two weeks together before the final repairs would be done and they'd be shipped off to opposite ends of the galaxy. Sasha was heading to the Imperial planet Viridian had relocated their cloning operation to. It would be a home base from which she would travel to various systems Viridian had a presence in, to help oversee the dismantling of the defunct corporation's assets and the care of the helpless young girls they had rescued from the industrial tissue regenerator farms.

Amanda's repeated requests to accompany her had been overruled. Apparently, Sasha's connection to the issue was just enough to make her a valuable asset, while Amanda -being the one who'd blown the lid on it to begin with- had a conflict of interest.

It was bullshit, plain and simple. But it was bullshit she had to accept, and so she and Sasha had spent their last two weeks together before their new jobs. Their training had taken place on Earth, so they rented a large flier with a bed and a head in the back and toured the planet, fitting in as much as they could in the time they had. They visited the ruins of humanity's homeworld, toured the great cities of the Empire and spent their nights in each other's arms, desperately making memories to tide them through the long assignments to come.

When their time was up, they returned and underwent the last upgrade Amanda hoped to get.

They replaced not just the Seven series components, but many others, as well, using cutting-edge Imperial technology to image the software onto the new parts in a process similar to that which the Transhumanist Collective used to upload their minds into the virtual environments they loved so much.

The old metabolic generators that had provided their electronics power were replaced with miniscule Matter-Antimatter reactors that required only a tiny fraction of the fuel of the originals. Their memory modules had been upgraded, giving them several hundred years worth of memories. Their BCIs had been swapped out for more complex ones that were tightly integrated into the rest of their systems, and the Behavioral Modules that regulated their State codes, as well as the core modules that contained their digital gray matter and personalities had been moved to new, tiny chips that ran even faster, giving them the ability to slow down time, from their perspective. It slowed down their movements as well, but was still a powerful ability.

They also discovered a forgotten ability: They could enable the State codes partially; sliding them halfway or a quarter of the way on and off. The Seven series components had turned on safeties that prevented this from being used, but with the repairs done, they turned back on. With the help of some ICIB programmers during their recovery, both women built software to manage the State codes for them, based on their intentions, as read by their new BCIs. The new ones were far more seamless, able to read their thoughts and understand their circumstances, as well as feed information directly to their brains without requiring them to listen to a disembodied voice or read glowing text in their field of view.

And then it was time to say goodbye. Both of them cried, bawling like children at the thought of not seeing each other for god knows how long. But they were adults, so they resolved to stay in touch, and to meet up at every opportunity. They agreed that either could drop in on the other with little or no warning, operational considerations be damned. They promised to send emails and videos, and then Sasha left on a military transport ship.

Amanda stayed on Earth a few more days to be briefed on her new assignment. She would be working with the IDF on the problem of this newly discovered alien species, the Hive. The Hive was busily conquering its way through Rhodanian space at the moment, and had been for the past few years. The Rhodanians -both of the nations known to humanity- were in shambles. The Empire had diplomatic ties to one nation and was rendering aid and running joint military operations, but the other, the nation responsible for horrifying raids into Terran space in years long past, was being left out to die.

Her job was to liase with a special forces unit of the IDF, to work with them while they conducted several recon strikes into newly conquered Hive territory, and then to take what they learned and turn it into actionable intelligence. To that end, she was sitting in an orbiter as it flew through stormy conditions on a Rhodanian-owned planet thousands of lightyears outside of human space.

It took thirty minutes to drop below the clouds, and then another forty to fly through howling winds and driving rain to their destination. They finally sat down on a tiny landing pad, at a tiny airport (not even a spaceport) in the middle of a vast wilderness of scrubby desert, currently in the middle of the monsoon season. Amanda bid her pilot farewell and wished him luck with his ascent. In turn, he wished her luck with her 'spy shit', and warned her not to piss off the team she would be working with. "I've heard stories, lady," he said, "about Operators who make 'above and beyond' their SOP, and if there's any truth to them, you'd better believe that's who they got to pull this shit off."

Amanda thanked him for his warning and disembarked. The rain was still pouring down, and it soaked her immediately. She knew already that three members of this team would be men, so she'd dressed appropriately. Her white top went transparent, betraying her lack of a bra and hopefully, giving them something to think about other than trying any tricks with her.

The relationship between the ICIB and the IDF hadn't been so hot these last few years, and field agents were warned to be on their toes when working with the military. Amanda hoped she wouldn't have any problems, but it never hurt to be sure.

She spotted four figures in unmarked IDF field uniforms with green berets stuffed in their back pockets, standing inside the only hangar and watching her. She jogged quickly over to meet them.

As she ran inside the hanger, she laughed. "I was *not* expecting to get soaked with rain in the middle of a desert!" she explained, flipping her wet hair back out of her face and forcing an embarrassed laugh.

One of the soldiers, a young man of obvious asian descent eyed her with interest, a small smile on his lips. "Lady, we haven't even been introduced yet, but I can already tell you I'm a huge fan of your bad decisions." He stuck a hand out in greeting and Amanda took it, smiling back with just a hint of playfulness in her eyes.

"John White," he said. "Aster," Amanda responded.

"Like the flower?" he asked. She nodded.

John leaned forward and whispered in her ear conspiratorially, "They're my favorite flower. Just so you know."

Amanda winked at him, but didn't say a word. This man's saccharine charms were already beginning to make her regret the decision to try and keep them on their heels. She turned to the others, holding out her hand. The sole woman took it first.

Amanda pegged her as a once-potential model who hadn't cared enough about her looks to make it. She had well-defined, delicate features, including a nose just striking enough to demand attention, and thick full lips. But she also had the remnants of childhood acne scarring her cheeks and forehead, and her eyes and the set of her mouth was hard, all business. Something about her seemed familiar, but Amanda couldn't place it. "Elizabeth Keppler," she said, shaking Amanda's hand. Her grip was firm, with hands like a robot's; thin, impossibly strong fingers wrapped in a rippling network of tendons and draped in thick veins.

The biggest one came next. He was built like a bodybuilder, but he had the face of an accountant, with deep-set, intelligent eyes and a smooth baritone voice. "Richard Isaacs."

Finally, Amanda turned to the one with the most stripes on his sleeves. He was a little over one point eight meters tall, and she'd eat her shoes if he weighed more than seventy five kilos. Like the woman, he didn't have an ounce of fat on him. He wore a genial smile on his face, but his eyes… He had the eyes of a killer, dead and haunted. Amanda's threat assessment climbed to 81% and her BCI opened up a fair portion of Flytrap, just in case.

"Jason Keppler," he said, his voice friendly enough, "Of the 105th SOG. I believe we're going to be working with you on this operation."

Dedication

This book is dedicated to my wife and children, first and foremost. Their patience with me coming home from work and writing instead of cooking dinner or playing Minecraft is part of what allowed me to finish this work. This book is also dedicated to all the readers of Jerry and the Goddesses on Reddit. If it weren't for all of you, I don't think I would have had the confidence to write this. Finally, I would like to extend a specific shoutout to the usernames of my two beta readers for the sequel to Operational Realities; JazzyJackal and Krichevskoy. You guys are amazing, and the only reason I didn't beg you to help me with this one is because I wanted to preserve the mysteries for you. I hope it's worth it.

About the Author

Matthew Aadland lives in South Florida with his wife, two kids and a dog. He's worked in the military, construction, sales, IT, engineering and software development as well as an embarrassingly diverse assortment of odd jobs, because he's still not sure what he wants to be when he grows up.

He enjoys writing, making music, painting, woodworking, leatherworking, painting miniatures, making dioramas, digital 3d modeling, modding and playing video games and whatever other hobbies happen to get hooks in his ADHD-addled brain this week.

If all of that sounds interesting, then I'm afraid I have bad news for you. He's really boring. Hence why he wrote a book about maladjusted people with serious issues doing amazing things. In Spaaaaaaace! This is his first book, so give him a break, okay? Yeesh, he knows he's not very good at this. He's trying.

9 798836 603632